"So you're the girl who ditched poor old Brooke."

Jarrah's penetrating gaze was accusing. "Threw him over because of a whim—that you'd prefer to forget the marriage bit and have a fun time drifting around the country. Brooke told me the whole story."

"I'll bet he did," Liz said bitterly. "How did you know it was me?"

"I couldn't miss with Brooke's description. A girl named Liz with a look of innocence and startling blue eyes. A girl you couldn't trust one inch because she'd let you down every time."

"How could you believe such a thing!" Liz protested. "He's lying to you. You don't know Brooke like I do!"

"Or you, come to that." Jarrah's sardonic grin enraged Liz. How could she possibly stay here knowing how he felt about her? And yet what did this stranger's opinion matter? Somehow, though, she knew that it did.

Gloria Bevan, though born in Australia, was raised in New Zealand where she now lives with her building inspector husband. They have three grown daughters. She has been writing stories for as long as she can remember and feels "there's a certain magic about writing even when the characters refuse to act the way I want them to." When not writing, she explores the many and varied exotic locations within reach of her suburban Auckland home.

Books by Gloria Bevan

HARLEQUIN ROMANCE

1809—CONNELLY'S CASTLE
1860—HIGH-COUNTRY WIFE
1923—ALWAYS A RAINBOW
2008—DOLPHIN BAY
2073—BACHELOR TERRITORY
2149—PLANTATION MOON
2224—FRINGE OF HEAVEN
2278—KOWHAI COUNTRY
2377—HALF A WORLD AWAY
2426—MASTER OF MAHIA
2455—EMERALD CAVE
2563—THE ROUSEABOUT GIRL
2618—GREEK ISLAND MAGIC
2713—SOUTHERN SUNSHINE

Golden Bay

Gloria Bevan

Harlequin Books

TORONTO • NEW YORK • LONDON
AMSTERDAM • PARIS • SYDNEY • HAMBURG
STOCKHOLM • ATHENS • TOKYO • MILAN

Original hardcover edition published in 1986
by Mills & Boon Limited

ISBN 0-373-02851-2

Harlequin Romance first edition August 1987

Printed in U.S.A.

CHAPTER ONE

Liz tossed down the spanner she had been using on the
terminals of her dust-coated old car, wiped the beads of
perspiration from her hot forehead with a grease-
smeared hand and tried once again to start the motor.
But there was no response to her efforts.

Frustratedly she glared at the battered vehicle
standing oh, so motionless in the clear bright sunshine.
Who would have believed, she told herself exasperatedly, that the old car that had behaved so well during her
days of touring through the New Zealand countryside
would have let her down in the loneliest spot she had
ever been in her life. A bush-filled gully where there was
no sign of civilisation, nothing but sheep-threaded hills
rising all around her—and the silence!

I guess I can't really blame old Hercules, she
acknowledged silently, lifting the bonnet of the car as a
signal that she was in need of help on the overgrown
track, not at the low price I paid for him! One thing, she
comforted herself, these back-country guys are pretty
well clued up when it comes to getting broken-down
vehicles back into action. Meanwhile all she could do
was to will herself to patience and wait until a motorist
happened along the dusty track.

Flinging herself down on the springy grass at the
roadside, she lay with face upturned to the translucent
blue above, hands crossed behind her head and long
strands of dark hair, glossy as the sheen on a tui's wing,
fanning out around her shoulders.

This is a funny way to spend your wedding day! Despite
her resolution to put the past behind her, her thoughts

drifted back. It had been a heat-hazy summer's day like this when she had first met Brooke. One thing was for sure, she told herself fiercely, never again would she fall a willing victim to the facile charm of an attractive stranger! She must have been out of her mind to mistake a romantic infatuation for the reality of a deep and lasting love affair.

From the day six weeks earlier when Brooke had arrived to take up the position of manager of her father's hill-country farm she had been attracted to the blond, good-looking stranger. And he told her he felt the same way about her.

Their shared interest in the world of show-jumping had formed a special bond between them, for Brooke, astride his grey thoroughbred Sabre, was a familiar figure in equestrian events held throughout the country. Then had come the triumph of his having been selected to represent New Zealand at the Horse Trials to be held at Badminton on the other side of the world. Liz's father's offer to advance Brooke the necessary funds to cover his air fares and living expenses in England had set the seal on his elation. 'Great!' His pleasant tones rang with excitement. 'I won't let you down,' he had promised his employer, 'you can be sure of that! I'll pay you back the money before long. After all,' he had flashed his engaging grin towards Liz, 'it's all in the family—or soon will be!'

All too soon had come the morning of Brooke's departure for the Wellington airport. The parting had been hard to bear, but she knew the trip to England was the culmination of all his hopes and dreams and, held close to his chest, she wished him all the luck in the world.

'You're my luck, my darling!' he had whispered against her lips. 'I'll be back before you realise it——Look why don't we set a date for the wedding right now? The week I arrive back from England? What do you say? Reckon you can jack up arrangements beforehand?'

'Why not?' She had snuggled closer to him.

'If only I didn't have to leave you.' His tones were husky with emotion. 'Nothing but the Trials would drag me away from you,' she could barely catch his low tones, 'and I haven't even given you an engagement ring.'

'What does it matter?' Mistily Liz had smiled up into his eyes. 'Just get back in time for the wedding——'

'As if I'd let anything in the world stop me!'

He had drawn her closer in his arms, covering her face and throat with passionate kisses. When at last he tore himself away she had run to climb the grassy hill behind the house, straining her eyes to catch a last glimpse of his car as it sped along the track leading to the main highway. All at once she couldn't see for the tears that misted her vision, and when she looked again Brooke had turned a bend in the road and passed out of sight. *I never dreamed that his leaving me could make the whole world seem so empty and meaningless*, she thought.

Idiot! she chided herself the next moment. The parting isn't for long. In a few weeks he'll be back and after that we won't be parted again—ever!

Slowly, slowly the days dragged by, and then at last it was time for Brooke to return. Even though he hadn't gained top honours in the overseas Horse Trials he had nevertheless acquitted himself well, returning to his native land in a blaze of publicity. Unexpectedly delayed by an air strike, he had arrived just in time for the wedding ceremony arranged in the small white timber church at the nearest township twenty miles distant.

The wedding was to be a small informal affair, for both Liz and Brooke were short on relatives, Brooke had only a stepbrother, he told Liz, a few years older than himself.

'What's he like?' Liz had asked, curious about anyone connected with Brooke.

'Don't ask me.' Brooke had shrugged away the enquiry. 'I scarcely know the guy, haven't seen him since we were kids. He was in the car-racing game for a while, made quite a name for himself on the racing circuits overseas, but a bad crash at Monaco put a finish to all that. You might know the name. Conway—Jarrah Conway.'

'Oh, I do! I used to read about all his wins in the newspapers. He was quite famous——'

'Was is the operative word,' he told her. 'After he got out of hospital he gave the racing car game away and took up land somewhere along the coast. Don't bother sending him an invitation to the wedding. I'll look up his address in the phone book and give him a buzz on the blower, put him into the picture about being best man on the big day.'

As for Liz, Aunt Rose was the only mother she had known. Years ago, when Liz's mother had been killed in a car crash on a lonely farm road, her sister-in-law had arrived at the farmhouse to care for the baby girl and had remained ever since to make a home for her widowed brother and his child.

Friends and neighbours, however, had received invitations to the quiet wedding that was to be followed by a small gathering of guests at Liz's home.

Only things hadn't worked out that way. Right from the moment when Brooke had walked into her home, Liz had sensed that something was very wrong. The moment that she and Brooke found themselves alone he had burst into speech, his eyes avoiding her gaze, his usual jaunty tones oddly hesitant. 'Look, I . . . the thing is, I couldn't write to you about this. I wanted to wait until I could tell you myself, let you down lightly—if I could.'

'Tell me what?' A dawning comprehension came into her eyes. 'You've met someone else, some other girl over there—that's it, isn't it?'

'Well . . .' He avoided her accusing look. 'Sorry about this love.' Such a tide of humiliation and shock swept her that she had difficulty in concentrating on his ragged tones. 'You know how it is,' he muttered, 'these things happen.'

The thought penetrated her numbed senses that he didn't sound at all sorry, rather relieved at having got an unpleasant duty over with. Liz wrenched her mind back to his low tones. 'Amelia and I—we were together all through the Trials and we clicked right from the word go. Believe me, this was the last thing I would have thought could happen when I left you to go overseas, but that's the way it is. You may as well have it straight——' Brooke drew a deep breath and hurried on in a rush of words. 'The way Amelia and I feel about each other, it wouldn't be fair to let you go through with arrangements. Not when——'

'You're in love with her!' Could that really be her own voice, so dull and expressionless? Liz recalled the masculine accents that were now tinged with satisfaction. 'You've guessed it. You must have heard of Amelia—Amelia James. She's made quite a name for herself overseas as an A-grade show-jumper.'

Liz said slowly, 'I've—read about her.' Across the screen of her mind flickered a picture she had recently come across in a horse and pony magazine, a photograph of the well-known English rider, Amelia James. A nondescript-looking girl, Liz had thought at the time, taking in the ungainly figure and hard mouth.

Amelia had been posed against the backdrop of the stately manor house that was her home. Not far distant,

immaculately kept fences enclosed neatly kept fields.
And in the extensive stables a groom was brushing
down Amelia's spirited white show-jumper, Moonlight.

'You'll be living in England, then?' Again came the
flat tones that seemed to Liz to belong to another girl
rather than to herself.

'That's the story.' Brooke's good-looking face had
lighted up. 'I knew you'd understand. Happens all the
time. No one's to blame—fact of life, that's all!' His
disparaging glance moved to the open window with its
vista of sun-dried slopes sweeping away to the misty
blue of distant hills.

'Will I ever be glad to get shot of this dump!' There
was an ugly twist to his full lips. 'From now on it's going
to be a whole new scene for me! No more being buried
alive in a hole like this, mucking around with horses all
my spare time, working like a galley-slave from dawn to
dark just to keep myself afloat financially. A man would
be a fool——' He broke off, and Liz saw a tide of brick-
red colour creep up beneath the smooth tan of his
cheeks. Hastily he made an attempt to cover the slip of
the tongue. 'Now don't get me wrong——'

'So that's it!' Shock and apathy in Liz's mind gave
way to a blazing anger. 'Now I know the reason why
you're keen on this English girl you've only known for a
few weeks! Why don't you come right out with it and
admit the truth? I'm right, aren't I?'

'Hell, no!' he blustered indignantly. 'What do you
take me for?' But the colour in his cheeks had deepened.
'If you're on about the money your father put up for me
to go over to the Trials, you can tell him for me he has no
need to worry on that score. It will all be taken care of.'

Liz felt sick. She said very low, 'You know I'm not
thinking about the loan.'

'You are now!' he threw at her. 'Well, you can forget

it! Your father will get it back, every single cent of it. He has only to wait——'

'You mean until after you're married to Amelia?' Liz despised herself for the taunting words, but they had slipped out before she could stop them.

Brooke's lips curved in a sneer. 'You are jealous of Amelia, aren't you?' After a moment he went on sulkily, 'I've told you I'm sorry about all this. I don't know what more you want me to say!' As she made no answer but stared back at him with bright accusing eyes he muttered tight-lipped, 'That's it, then! No sense in prolonging the agony!' Abruptly he turned on his heel and flung out of the room.

Liz stood still, staring after him, her eyes sparkling with anger. All at once a monstrous thought crossed her mind. Could it be that all along she had been mistaken in Brooke's true character? Was it possible that his well-cut features, fine physique and blond good looks had blinded her to the type of man he really was?

He had a way with words when it suited his purpose. The conviction was swiftly growing in her mind that he was a man who relied on his attention-getting appearance and smooth tongue to secure for himself the good things in life.

He hadn't long held the position of manager of her father's property. Supposing—she caught her breath at the appalling thought that had shot into her mind— Brooke had hoped that by marrying into the family he could secure for himself far greater financial rewards than he could expect as a manager of the property? She was an only child and following a recent near-fatal heart attack her father would probably never again be able to return to gruelling physical toil.

She caught herself up, horrified at the direction in which her thoughts were drifting. Brooke couldn't, he wouldn't—and yet ... In spite of herself the ugly suspicion persisted. Had she been a mere tool for his ambitions? Was Brooke an opportunist, a man who having gained the love and trust of an affluent woman, was now anxious to put the old love out of his life without a tinge of compunction or regret? Deep down where it counted she knew it was the truth, So why did the knowledge hurt so much? Her own stupid pride? Because she must force herself to endure the unspoken sympathy of friends and relatives, invent some plausible excuse to explain the last-minute cancellation of wedding plans.

It was later that morning when Brooke made a brief visit to the house, and after a few words with his employer, he had jumped into his car with its still unopened suitcases and driven away.

Liz, watching from the window, thought angrily that it meant nothing at all to Brooke that he was leaving her father, already short of labour, in desperate straits at a busy season of the year.

The blazing sense of outrage that Brooke had sparked in her sustained her all the time she spent on the telephone contacting friends and relatives, caterers and the vicar of the tiny church she and Brooke had chosen for their wedding.

'Surprise! Surprise!' She tried to make her voice light and carefree. 'Brooke and I have decided to call off the wedding! You know how involved he is in show-jumping, and now with the titles he's won he can't wait to get back to England.'

After the first moment of stunned silence friends were quick to offer criticism. 'What's wrong with the man! All that publicity, it must have gone to his head.'

Or his heart. Liz said the words silently, shying away from any suggestion of sympathy. That she couldn't take.

In the following days Aunt Rose proved a tower of

strength at a time when Liz most needed her. She was
grateful to the older woman as cheerfully and tactfully
her aunt dealt with the endless telephone messages,
relieving Liz of the pain and humilation of going over
and over a situation she wished only to forget. It was
almost, she told herself in surprise, as though her aunt
were relieved rather than dismayed at the sudden
change of plan. All at once Liz wondered if Aunt Rose
with her shrewd common sense had not been entirely
taken in by Brooke's smooth talk and flashing smile.

Not like her father. A man of few words, he said little
on learning of his daughter's shattered romance, beyond
a quietly spoken, 'You've had a lucky escape there, girl!'

Liz had sent him a tremulous smile. 'I know, Dad, I
know.' Inwardly she was thinking that her father's
brooding angry eyes showed all too clearly that the
betrayal by a man who he had both liked and trusted
had gone deep with him.

Now she was glad of the physical activity that helped
to keep the niggling thoughts at bay. For in the
following few days she worked long hours, shifting
sheep from one paddock to another, riding down to the
creek to check the water pump or taking the sheep-
threaded hills on horseback, her gaze ever altered for
the sight of a cast sheep or a trailing wire fence wire. At
the end of the week an experienced farm manager
arrived at the property to fill the vacancy left by Brooke,
and it was then that Liz decided on taking a tour of the
back country. She had only just begun her six weeks'
break from schoolteaching and a summer motor tour
was something she had long planned to take.

Her father and aunt were enthusiastic over the idea.
'It's the best thing you could do,' they encouraged. 'To
get right away from here and forget everything that's
happened.'

With a start she came back to the present. Right at

this moment, she told herself wryly, she wasn't so sure about the touring trip being such a great notion. If someone didn't come along this lonely bush track to rescue her before nightfall—— And then she heard it! The unmistakable sound of an approaching vehicle.

Jumping to her feet, she stood waiting at the roadside and the next minute a truck swung around a tree-lined bend and bore down on her.

Soon, to the accompaniment of loudly called greet-ings and goodnatured remarks from the group of men in the truck, the dust-coated vehicle drew up alongside her. Liz's lightning glance took in the masculine figures, husky-looking types with brawny shoulders under black sweat-shirts, faces and arms sun-darkened to a coppery tan and sheathed knives swinging in leather holsters from low-slung leather belts. A shearing gang, she thought, probably on their way to fulfilling a contract at one of the vast sheep stations further along the coast.

'You having a spot of trouble, miss?' A massively built Maori man leaped down from the driver's seat and came strolling leisurely towards her. 'What's the problem.' A friendly grin lighted his goodnatured-looking face. 'Need some help?'

'Do I ever!' Liz responded in her soft, eager tones. 'I——'

'Hi, Liz!'

'Greg!' She swung around in surprise to face the slightly built fair-haired young man with smiling grey eyes who had dropped down from the truck and had come to stand at her side.

'The last time I saw you,' he grinned, 'was in your dad's shearing shed one day last summer. You brought the tea and scones down to the gang, remember?' Before she could answer he ran on in his friendly tones, 'What are you doing so far away from home? And all on your lonesome too!'

She tossed him a cheeky grin, dimples flickering in the apricot tan of her cheeks. 'What do *you* think? Waiting for you to come along the road and rescue me of, course. What took you so long?'

Her words were drowned by the noisy comments of the shearing gang. Clearly appreciative of a break in the monotony of a long and dusty trip, the men crowded around her.

'My car let me down,' Liz explained. 'It stopped—just like that!' She lifted small tanned hands in an expressive gesture. 'Honestly, you wouldn't believe! One minute I was going along fine, admiring the scenery, then wham! The car stopped dead and there wasn't even a flicker of life in the engine.'

'Let's take a look-see.' Work-roughened hands lifted higher the bonnet of the old car and sun-weathered masculine faces peered inside. Greg climbed into the driver's seat and under the shouted directions of his work-mates, pulled various levers and pressed switches, but it was all to no avail.

Presently a chorus of deep voices gave their considered opinion as to the the cause of the breakdown, Liz, listening intently, gathered that the team was in agreement concerning the cause of the car's breakdown. 'Battery's shot,' they announced. 'Finished.'

'But it can't be!' Liz protested incredulously. 'The salesman at the car yard where I bought Hercules told me there was a brand new battery——'

The statement drew shouts of derisive laughter.

'Well, nearly new,' she conceded, and the next moment became aware that the words had sparked yet another burst of scornful guffaws.

'Where are you heading for anyway?' Greg enquired in the modulated accent that she remembered as out of keeping with his black sweat-shirt, tattered shorts and bare tanned feet. The thought crossed her mind that he

had a very nice smile and there was something
definitely heartwarming in the expression of his
friendly grey eyes. He really must be very much stronger
than one would imagine, judging by his slight physique,
she mused, to sustain the long hours and gruelling
physical toil in the steamy summer heat of the shearing
sheds.

Aloud she answered lightly, 'Just touring around,
having a look at this and that! Right now I'm looking
for some place where I can put up for the night and
arrange to get my old bus back on the road. Any offers?'
Her smile included the gang of men.

As the clamour of voices echoed around her she took
it there was no problem in that direction. The team
would be glad to drop her off at the first homestead they
came to along the road.

'You're so lucky,' Greg told her. 'It's only by the
merest chance that we decided to take this short cut
through the gully to cut out a couple of hours' driving.
Since the new road went through last year this is just a
wild goat track. I wouldn't give much for your chances
of anyone else showing up here tonight, or tomorrow
either for that matter! Not to worry, though. We're due
in the morning at a station further south, got to get an
early start there tomorrow. You know how it is when the
team is booked in for a week's shearing and the good
weather holds.'

'Just drop me off at the first homestead we come
to——' Liz broke off, a worried frown creasing her
forehead. 'But what about my car?'

'No problem,' a brawny member of the gang assured
her. 'There are big holdings around this part of the
country with swags of staff. The boss'll send a man back
here to pick up your old bus and with a bit of luck they'll
have their own mechanic on the payroll.'

Liz let out her breath on a sigh of relief. 'Sounds wonderful!'

'Ready now, miss?' came the soft accents of the Maori truck driver as he swung open the door of the cab.

'More than ready!' She climbed up the high step and seated herself beside him.

Soon the truck continued along the narrow winding track, a cloud of dust rising behind the vehicle. The shearers burst into song, their strong male voices harmonising in a popular melody of the day.

Liz was only half listening to the relaxed tones of the driver as he described the various stations where the team had worked this summer, her gaze roving over the parched, sheep-dotted slopes rising around them.

Presently they were climbing a steep slope where the road twisted and turned endlessly, affording vistas of rolling countryside. And still she could glimpse no sign of any dwelling. It was a long time later that she became aware of the dull roar of waves breaking on an unseen shore and in her nostrils was the salty tang of the sea. A weathered signpost lurching at a precarious angle suddenly loomed to her sight and she caught a glimpse of the faded black lettering, 'Hauturu Station'.

The next moment they swung over the hilltop and were lurching down a track soft with drifting sand, zigzagging down the steep station land that dropped to meet the blue waters of the Pacific Ocean.

Liz's fascinated gaze swept the expanse of sand that formed part of a magnificent sweep of coastline. Then her eyes shifted to a rambling old homestead with its wide bay windows facing the sea and creeper-hung verandahs looked lived-in and somehow welcoming.

Bushes of Bird-of-Paradise with their vivid splashes of purple and orange and blue flowers studded lawns sloping down to meet the sands of the sheltered bay below. Soon they were sweeping past cabbage trees clinging tenaciously to dried slopes and then they were approaching sea-level, clattering over a cattle stop and following a winding track leading towards the homestead.

Liz's gaze took in the scattered outbuildings, their red timbers mellowed over the years. They passed a woolshed, stockyards and drafting pens. A corral was shaded by tall macrocarpa trees and near the open doors of stables, stock horses stood already saddled waiting for their riders.

In the garages a man wearing oil-stained overalls was working on a farm tractor. At sight of the approaching truck he straightened, responding with a friendly wave of his hand to Liz's smile of greeting. 'Right at this moment,' she confided to the driver seated at her side, 'that mechanic happens to be the most important man in my life!'

He threw her a sideways grin. 'I know what you mean.'

Presently they swept past two neatly kept timber bungalows surrounded by smooth green lawns. From a gateway a blonde young woman holding a baby in her arms smilingly acknowledged the toot-toot of the truck driver. Liz guessed that the white-painted bungalows were the homes of the married shepherds working at Hauturu.

The curving driveway seemed to go on for ever, but at last they went past a line of sheepdogs chained to their kennels and drew up at the foot of a flight of wide stone steps leading up to the sun-dappled verandah of the old kauri homestead.

At that moment a Land Rover pulled up beside them and the driver called from the vehicle, 'Looking for me? Sorry, mate,' he was eyeing the Maori driver of the truck, 'looks like you've got your lines crossed somewhere. I've got a team of shearers working in the shed right now.'

Liz saw a dark-haired young man, lean, muscular and good-looking. He had a relaxed air and a laconic manner of speaking, so why, she wondered, did she get this impression of latent strength and power lying just beneath the surface? He must be the boss of the outfit, she just knew it!

'Not to worry,' one of the shearers called, grinning. 'We're not planning on putting up here. Just called in to drop off a delivery.'

'Delivery?' The man in the Land Rover raised thickly-marked black eyebrows. 'I don't get it. You've made a blue somewhere——'

There was a burst of masculine laughter. 'No mistake!' a chorus of male voices answered.

'Okay, then.' Plainly, Liz thought, the boss of Hauturu was becoming impatient. 'Let's have it!' he said shortly. 'Whatever it is you've got for me.'

Guffaws of laughter greeted his enquiry. 'You'd be surprised! Just something we picked up on the road on the way here.'

'Don't listen to them!' Liz made to leap down from the cab and in an instant Greg was out of the truck and helping her down the high step, holding her in his arms a trifle longer than was necessary before setting her down on the driveway.

'This is Liz,' he told the stranger, 'and she happens to be in a spot of trouble. Her car broke down on the road miles away from here and we offered to give her a lift and drop her off at the first station homestead we hit on the way. All she wants is a bed for the night.'

'Is that right?' Something in the cool disapproving way in which the boss—he must be the boss—was regarding her, not to mention the guarded note in his rich masculine tones, was getting under Liz's skin. 'That's no problem,' he was saying, 'there's plenty of room in the house.' His tones were curiously aloof and uneasy thoughts raced though Liz's mind.

Could he have some utterly mistaken ideas, she thought indignantly, concerning a girl who arrived in the truck with a shearing gang? Maybe he didn't accept the explanation Greg had given him. Did he think——? What was he thinking? She tried to gather her confused thoughts together. Maybe if she avoided direct contact with those penetrating hazel eyes of his that seemed to look right through you . . .

It worked, she told herself the next minute, it really worked! For now her voice was bright and confident. She heard herself saying in her soft eager young tones, 'I'd be so grateful if you could put me up for the night. I waited for hours—well, it seemed like hours—at the side of the road hoping someone would come along. So if you could——'

His dispassionate glance met her gaze. She couldn't avoid his eyes for ever. 'Like I said, there's rooms to spare in the house and Mrs Malloy, she's my house-keeper, is used to the odd stranger dropping in for a night's shelter.'

His impersonal tones chilled her. How was it possible, she asked herself in dismay, for a man who was young and wildly attractive in appearance to have contrived to make the conventional words of welcome sound so off-putting? Deliberately so, she wouldn't wonder! Her blue eyes glowed with resentment and she whispered fiercely to Greg, 'There must be *somewhere* else where you can drop me. Another homestead further along the road?'

'Sorry,' his regretful tones reached her, 'but this is it. End of the journey. Last stop on the road. There's just nowhere else, not today anyway.'

Liz had an uneasy suspicion that the brief exchange of words had been overheard by the boss. At that moment the driver leaned from the cab. 'Right, we're off, then!' She felt the warm grip of Greg's hand on her arm. 'Look,' he said urgently, 'when can I see you again? I——'

'Break it up, Greg! We've got to hit the road!' The shouts of his mates in the truck cut off what Greg had been about to say and reluctantly he turned away.

'See you!' A chorus of voices echoed around Liz as the truck turned in the driveway.

'Bye.' She lifted a hand in a gesture of farewell. 'And thanks for all your help. See you next time I get stranded in the never-never between here and there!'

'That we should be so lucky!' The cheerful male voices drifted back to her. Greg was still waving to her as the vehicle swung into the long tree-lined driveway leading out to the main highway.

As Liz turned away she became aware of her companion's deep tones. 'You'd better come into the house.' You could tell by his couldn't-care-less-about-her tone of voice, she told herself, that he wasn't one little bit interested in her movements. The thought sparked her to say spiritedly, 'I'm sorry to have to trouble you, but there was just nowhere else to go.'

'No trouble,' came the cool rejoiner, 'my pleasure.'

'*Pleasure*!' She threw him a disbelieving glance. 'Somehow I get the feeling——' Her voice trailed into silence, for as she looked resentfully up into the strong masculine face, thoughts of quite a different nature went racing through her mind. Sensitively moulded lips, a deeply cleft chin, deep smile lines running down each side of his sun-bronzed face. An interesting face, enigmatic and exciting. She had to admit that he was wildly attractive in a tough, tanned sort of way. Not over-tall, yet she sensed an aura of masculine confidence and steely strength in his lithe muscular body.

There was about him an unmistakable air of authority. Not a man to accept evasions or deceit, not with those implacable hazel eyes. All at once it seemed terribly important that he should understand the true facts of her arrival here. Just to make certain that he should be under no misapprehensions concerning her, she lifted her small square chin and summoned her brightest smile. 'I guess you're wondering where I've come from?'

He shrugged wide shoulders beneath his cotton shirt and his cool tones were like a dash of cold water flung in her face. 'We'll talk later, shall we?'

Too incensed to answer, Liz accompanied him in an angry silence as they climbed the worn stone steps crowded on either side with flowering bushes.

His dispassionate tones broke the silence. 'Where did you leave your car?'

Liz choked down the hot words that had risen to her lips. It was no use. In her own interests she had no choice but to answer him. She forced her voice to an impersonal note. 'It's about two hours' drive away from here, maybe a mile from the turn-off at the main highway. An old bush road that isn't used much these days, so the shearers told me.'

'I know the place. I'll send a man over to collect your car in the morning. That suit you?'

She caught her lip with her teeth. 'Not really. I was hoping,' she said worriedly, 'to get back on the road sooner than that.'

'Not a chance.' His authoritative tones brooked no

argument in the matter. 'I can put you up for the night
and when I get your bus over here I'll get the mechanic
to give it the once-over. If he's got the necesssary parts
for a repair job in the shed, that is.'

He didn't appear to notice, she thought angrily, that
she had made no answer to his offer.

Soon they were crossing the open verandah where the
air was drenched with the fragrance of pink jasmine
blossoms that starred the vines cascading over beams
and posts. Then he was ushering her in to an open
doorway and along a wide carpeted passage.

'Is that you, Jay?' A short plump woman of middle
age with a cluster of fluffy blonde curls around her face
stopped short at sight of them. Her low-cut sunfrock
revealed a freckled throat and shoulders and her round
face was flushed and beaded with perspiration. As if,
Liz thought, the older woman had come from bending
over a range in the kitchen,

'Mrs Molly Malloy, this is Liz,' came the laconic
masculine tones.

'Nice to meet you, my dear.' The housekeeper was
wiping her damp pink face with a handkerchief. She
looked hot and uncomfortable but her smile, Liz
decided, was warm and friendly.

'Liz got herself stranded on the old back road through
the gully,' the boss was saying, 'you know the way it
happens.'

'Should do,' the housekeeper responded drily, 'considering the folk who land up here for shelter when their
car or caravan or whatever has let them down in that
godforsaken spot. It's no bother at all to put you up,' she
assured Liz, 'not a scrap.'

You could tell by the warmth in Mrs Malloy's voice,
Liz thought, that here was one person who meant what
she said when it came to welcoming a guest. She
brought her mind back to the cheerful feminine tones.

'You'll be wanting to take a shower before the meal
after that long trip over rough roads. Come with me and
I'll show you to your room.'

'I'll see you later.' The boss's tones lacked any
particular inflection. The next moment he had turned
away.

To Liz's travel-weary eyes, the room to which she was
led appeared infinitely fresh and inviting. A salty
breeze from the sea fluttered filmy curtains at wide open
windows. Fluffy natural-coloured sheepskin rugs lay on
the stained timber floor and the furniture consisted of
an old-fashioned bureau, a wardrobe, and twin beds
covered with freshly laundered lilac-coloured spreads.

The housekeeper's twinkling blue eyes took in Liz's
lack of hand luggage, her dust-stained jeans and grease-
spotted shirt.

'In case you're interested,' she said with a smile,
'you'll find spare garments in the bureau drawers. So if
you feel like a change of clothing or a nightgown, just
feel free to help yourself to what you need. There's
plenty of choice, from rainproof jackets to jodhpurs and
bikinis.' Her gaze ran over Liz's small slim figure. 'Your
size too. I've a niece who lives in town but spends her
holidays here and she likes to keep spares handy for the
next time she comes to stay. You'll find the bathroom
next door,' the kindly tones ran on. 'Wait, I'll bring you
some towels.' She was back with Liz almost at once.
'Just come along to the dining room when you're ready.
Dinner isn't until seven.'

'It's very good of you,' Liz said gratefully.

'Nonsense! It's no bother at all!' The warmth in the
blue Irish eyes underlined the sincerity of the conventional words.

After enduring the heat and dust of the long day the
warm shower was bliss to Liz. With an effort she forced
herself to put on once again her travel and grease-

stained clothing. She was too much in debt to everyone already. Nothing would induce her to make use of the garments the housekeeper had so thoughtfully put at her disposal. Liz could well imagine that man's look of satirical displeasure at the sight of her wearing clothes belonging to his housekeeper's niece. If only, she thought on a sigh, she didn't have to come in contact with the boss again!

Yet later when she made her way into the panelled dining room with its massive old kauri tables and chairs she was scarcely aware of others in the room, her gaze straying directly to the man who stood by the dresser that served as a cocktail cabinet, as he attended to drinks.

As she looked at him, freshly shaven, his thick dark hair still damp from the shower and wearing a cream-coloured body shirt and fawn cords, the thought ran through her mind that he looked more attractive than ever—and very much the man in control of his vast estates. Why not? He was, wasn't he? At that moment he swung around and for an electric moment their glances meshed and held. Those alive-looking hazel eyes, she thought dazedly, seemed to have the power to mesmerise her. With an effort of will, she wrenched her glance aside.

'What'll you have, Liz?' His impersonal tones jerked her back to reality.

'Me? Oh, just a sherry, please.'

'One sherry coming up!'

He crossed the room to hand her the drink in its crystal glass. The next moment Liz found Mrs Malloy at her side and presently the housekeeper was making the newcomer known to other guests in the room. Liz gathered that the middle-aged man with the weathered skin and quiet voice was Red, the head shepherd. The dark nuggety-looking man with a crushing hand-grip

was the local vet. Two young men wearing casual gear
who appeared to be enjoying themselves immensely
were a television crew who were staying the night at the
homestead after researching a programme featuring
historical sheep stations of New Zealand. A pale,
bearded young man told her he was a hunter who had
been reported as missing for the past two days. Lost in
heavy bush, he had only this morning found his way
back to civilisation.

As the meal progressed Liz tried to fit names to faces,
but it didn't really matter, she told herself, seeing that
her time here was so transitory. She was thankful to the
men seated around the table whose anecdotes and
laughter saved her from having to talk with the boss.
Always supposing, she reminded herself wryly, that he
deigned to talk with her!

Despite the circumstances that had brought her here,
Liz found herself enjoying the excellent meal that Mrs
Malloy had provided. Later the housekeeper carried a
tray of coffee mugs into the lounge and everyone moved
through the high archway dividing the two rooms. In a
swift glance around her Liz took in the long shadowy
room with its beamed ceiling and faded Persian rugs on
the polished floor. Long picture windows faced the
ocean and caught the last rays of a spectacular flame
and tangerine sunset. Guns were mounted over the
mantel and on the wall hung a portrait of the original
owner of the historic property. A wedding photograph
of bride and groom in their old-fashioned garments held
Liz's fascinated gaze, for the groom bore a startling
resemblance to the present owner of the station. Both
men had the same *vital* look, she found herself thinking,
the same heart-stopping appearance. Swiftly she caught
herself up, aghast at the direction in which her thoughts
were drifting, and tried to concentrate her attention on
the scene around her.

Before long she slipped away to the kitchen, a spacious modernised room painted in sunshiny tonings of primrose yellow where the walls were lined with gleaming sink benches, a fridge and a massive deep-freeze cabinet.

'Let me help you!' Liz whipped a teatowel from the rail and approached the housekeeper, who was standing at the sink.

'Thanks, love, I wouldn't mind a helping hand.' Mrs Malloy was plunging her hands in a froth of detergent in the soft rainwater in the basin. 'When I first came here to keep house for Jay he had an automatic dishwashing machine installed in the kitchen, but I told him I couldn't be bothered with it and he could send it right back to the shop!'

Liz was drying a plate. 'You'd best make the most of my offer,' she said with a smile, 'it will probably be my only night here.' And added under her breath, *With a bit of luck!*

CHAPTER TWO

THAT evening Liz went to her room early, selecting a light novel from the shelf above her head before slipping into bed and pulling the sheet over her, the only covering needed on this hot night. Somehow, though, she couldn't concentrate on the story. There were too many other more important matters crowding her mind, like the boss! Could it be because of the unfavourable impression she had made on him that the strong masculine features rose on the screen of her mind in place of the printed words?

The next moment a sharp rap on the door made her glance up expectantly. 'Come in, Mrs Malloy!' she called.

But it was a man's dark head that appeared around the lintel and the next minute the boss had let himself into the room and closed the door behind him.

Liz's heart was beating unevenly and as he came striding purposefully towards her she drew the sheet protectively around her bare rounded shoulders. If only she had availed herself of the housekeeper's offer of a nightgown from the bureau drawer! Now it was too late. All she could do was to slide down in the bed and glare defiantly up into his dark intimidating face.

'You can relax.' His sardonic gaze mocked her. 'If that's what's on your mind.'

'I'm not worrying!' she threw back at him with attempted bravado. For some reason she couldn't fathom, his contemptuous appraising look had been humiliating rather than reassuring to her bruised ego.

She pulled her mind back to the deep masculine tones.

'I'm here for a purpose, wanted to get something straightened out—— Don't get me wrong,' his magnetic hazel eyes seemed to be staring right through her and she couldn't sustain his gaze, 'I've no objection to putting you up for a day or two and I'll see that your car is taken care of. I'll get my mechanic to give it a good going over so it will be top order when you take off again.'

Liz's soft lips were pressed tightly together and she threw him an angry glance. He was making it sound as though she were of no more importance around his property than a piece of machinery to be transported here and there at his convenience!

'Thanks very much!' She forced the words through stiff lips.

It seemed, however, that sarcasm was wasted on him. He continued to stare down at her, strong and dominant, making her feel very much at a disadvantage, almost—at his mercy.

She said spiritedly, 'What *are* you here for, then? Do I take it that this visit to my room indicates you want payment of some kind in advance? Because I'm telling you right now that if you're expecting favours, financial or otherwise, you're way out of line!'

Dismissing her words as of no importance, he dropped down to seat himself on the bed, hazel eyes probing her flushed face. 'Tell me, Liz—Elizabeth, I take it. Elizabeth who?'

'Stuart,' she said, puzzled by the intensity of his gaze. 'Why? Does it matter?'

He didn't answer directly. 'Stuart,' he murmured thoughtfully. 'It's a common enough name, and yet . . .' All at once his eyes narrowed. 'You don't happen to come from a little place called Manuki, do you?'

'Actually I do, but I don't see that it has anything to do——'

'Quite a coincidence,' he commented drily. His richly masculine tones were ice-cold, his expression dark and forbidding. 'I had an idea who you might be when you showed up here, but I thought my name would have rung a bell with you.'

'I can't think why,' she said with spirit. 'I've never set eyes on you before in my life!'

His intent gaze didn't leave her face. 'But you've heard my name mentioned?'

'No!' But a horrifying suspicion was taking root in her mind. 'Should I have?'

'Jarrah Conway?'

Conway! Liz's thoughts rioted in confusion. Oh God, she cried inwardly, don't let it be him! Not Brooke's stepbrother!

'So you're the girl who ditched poor old Brooke at the last moment!' His penetrating gaze was sharp and accusing. 'Threw him over because of a whim that you'd prefer to forget the marriage bit and have a fun time drifting around the country, free as a bird. Tough luck for Brooke, but what did you care? You'd be miles away enjoying yourself the way you wanted—don't bother with the cover-up,' his harsh tones flayed her as she opened her lips in protest, 'because it won't wash, not with me! I had a note from Brooke telling me not to come north because there wasn't to be a wedding after all. He let me in on the whole story——'

'I'll bet he did,' she said with bitter irony. 'How did you know—it was me?'

'I couldn't miss, with the description I got from Brooke. A girl named Liz with a look of innocence and startling blue eyes. A girl you couldn't trust an inch because she'd let you down every time!'

'How *could* you believe such a thing!' she burst out. To her chagrin she could feel the hot colour flooding her cheeks. 'Look,' she cried, 'he's lying to you. I can explain——'

'Don't trouble yourself!' His voice cut like a whiplash. 'You're wasting your time trying to pull the wool over my eyes. You haven't a hope in hell!'

As she looked up into the hard set face above, hope died in her. What was the use of trying to make him see the truth? She said very low, 'If only you'd listen to me.'

'Any particular reason why I should?'

'Yes, there is!' she cried defiantly. 'You don't know Brooke like I do——'

The sardonic lift of his well-shaped lips lacked any suggestion of humour. 'Or you, come to that!'

All at once she could see the way in which his mind was working. He might just as well have voiced his suspicions of her out loud. A girl who had arrived in a truck with a gang of shearers. A girl who had told the boss she had only met the team a few hours previously yet was already on familiar terms with one of the gang.

The injustice of his attitude swept over her. 'You won't give me a chance to explain, will you?' She made an angry movement to sit up, then, suddenly aware of her nakedness, clutched the sheet around her. 'You'd believe anything, wouldn't you!' Her eyes were blazing with indignation and anger. 'Anything that Brooke told you about me rather than letting me tell you the truth!'

'*Your* version of the truth!' he retorted. 'And haven't you forgotten something? He happens to be my brother——'

'Stepbrother, you mean!' Liz was determined to go down fighting even if the battle were lost. 'He told me when we were making out the wedding invitations that

he'd only met you once, and that was years ago.' Not
that he hadn't still an eye to the main chance, she
thought cynically. Brooke wanted his only relative to
continue to think well of him. If his marriage to Amelia
didn't take place he might want a loan in future.

'And just how well,' drawled the richly masculine
tones, 'do I know you? Why should I take your word for
what happened between you rather than his?'

As she met his implacable look she was swept by a
sense of frustration and anguish. 'It's not *fair*!' she
exploded breathlessly. 'It wasn't the way you're thinking! If you'd only let me tell you——'

'Tell me what? A pack of lies?' Ice dripped in his
deep tones. 'Brooke wrote to me at the time about how
broken up he was——'

'Broken up?' Liz cried incredulously. 'About what?'

'About the treatment you handed out to him, of
course!'

She stared up at him, blue eyes sparkling with
indignation. 'Brooke all broken up about me? You've
got to be joking! You don't know the half of it if you
believe that. Tell me,' she demanded hotly, 'just what
did Brooke tell you in his letter?'

'That you'd ditched him at the last moment before the
wedding.'

'What else?' Her voice was dangerously quiet.

'And that you'd handed him the bad news when he
was feeling on top of the world after his successes at the
Badminton Horse Trials. It was typical of the sort of girl
you are, he told me, to pull a mean trick like that. He
was lucky, he thought, to have found out just in time the
type of girl he was marrying.'

'And you believed him! Trust men,' Liz threw at him
sharply, 'to stick together!'

'Naturally I believed him! That kind of behaviour is typical of your sex!'

Her eyes shot sparks of anger. 'I take it,' she taunted. 'that you rate yourself as some sort of expert when it comes to women!'

'I have my reasons.' There was a bitter twist to his mouth. 'I happen to have first-hand knowledge of how Brooke is feeling right now.' She had to strain her ears to catch the low words. 'I've been down that road myself.'

Liz opened her lips to speak, then closed them again. What could he mean? Then something clicked in her mind. Brooke telling her that his stepbrother had been a crack racing car driver until an accident on the racing track had ended his career. Funny how a newspaper report of the crash had stayed in her mind although it had all happened at least three years ago.

The internationally famous New Zealand racing car driver had been at the peak of his career when while competing at a Monaco Grand Prix his Formula 1 had flipped on a bend and he had been thrown out on to the track, badly hurt. The report had made mention of Jarrah's fiancée, a local girl, who had terminated the couple's wedding plans immediately on learning of Jarrah's near-fatal injury on the track. A long period in hospital, however, had resulted in his almost miraculous recovery.

The ball was in her court and she was determined to make the best use of her advantage. 'Now I see what's behind all this—this unfairness towards me!' She was aware that her impassioned tones were rising out of control, but the injustice of his snap judgment of her was goading her beyond the limits of endurance. 'So that's it!' she cried triumphantly. 'You're blaming me just because of what that other girl did to you! Ann, her name was, wasn't it? Refusing to hear my side of

the story, taking out your frustrations on me just
because——' She stopped short, appalled at the
accusation into which her anger had betrayed her.

She saw a muscle twitch in his cheek and knew that
her words had hit a nerve. Strangely, though, she felt no
sense of triumph in her victory but only an odd sense of
regret.

'Now that we've got a few things sorted out——'
There was a white tinge around his mouth and she
sensed that his carefully controlled tones concealed a
blazing anger. 'I'm off!' His cool eyed glance raked her
unmercifully. 'Sharp-tongued women don't attract me!'

At the doorway he paused to glance back at her. 'By
the way, in case you're wondering, our arrangement still
stands. You'll get your car back. Let Mrs Malloy know if
you need anything.'

Liz was silent, looking after him as he left the room.

Despite the hot night she was shivering and for a long
time she lay awake, staring into the darkness, listening
to the old grandfather clock in the hallway as it chimed
away the hours. Of all the places that she could have
come to for shelter, that it should be Jarrah Conway's
station! I couldn't possibly come to terms with a guy like
that, she told herself, yet somehow I've got to stay here.
Pray God it won't be for longer than a day!

In the morning when she awoke from a restless sleep
she was unaware of her surroundings, only of pale rays
of sunshine slanting over her face. The next minute
realisation of the events of the previous day returned
with a rush to her mind and the pleasure of finding
herself in the tastefully furnished room died away.

How could she endure staying here, she thought
desperately, dependent on Jarrah Conway's reluctant
hospitality, knowing the way he felt about her? Close on
the thought came another. What else can I do? I'm

trapped here in his home, of all places in the world!

To escape the worrying thoughts she jumped out of bed and parting the window curtains looked out at the eastern sky flushed with sunrise. Her gaze moved to the sea, glittering and flashing in the sunshine as though a giant hand had scattered myriad silver dollars on the tossing waves. One way to forget the problems that bedevilled her, especially her most pressing problem of all, Jarrah Conway, was to take an early morning dip in the sparkling sea. At this early hour there would be no one about in the sheltered bay. Already she could feel the exhilarating slap of crisp salt water against her skin. If only she had brought her swimsuit with her. But wait, hadn't Mrs Malloy mentioned something about a spare bikini in a bureau drawer? A minute later she was pulling from a tangle of garments a primrose-yellow bikini that looked as though it might fit her. Well, near enough for a solo morning dip!

I wouldn't mind borrowing it just for once. Liz reasoned away her resolution not to avail herself of anything belonging to *his* home. So long as he doesn't see me, she told herself, and there's no danger of that, because the boss as well as the men working on the station are sure to be out working somewhere in the hills around Hauturu. I just couldn't bear Jarrah Conway to recognise this bikini as belonging to his housekeeper's niece, to have to meet that horrible sardonic look he seems to keep just for me!

Soon she was letting herself silently out of the back door and making her way through a porch cluttered with men's jackets, sun-hats, riding boots, whips and gumboots. Then she was outside in the incredible clarity of the morning, running over the dew-wet grass of the sloping lawn and down to an expanse of golden sand, cool to the touch of her bare feet.

Her black hair streamed behind sun-tanned shoulders as she sped down the damp shoreline and plunged into the cool tingling force of the tossing sea. At that moment a great curling wave came surging towards her and she found herself tossed into the foaming trough of the breaker, her feet losing their hold on the shifting sands beneath.

Gasping for breath, she surfaced, then waded out into deeper water to stand poised for the onslaught of another wall of glassy green as it thundered towards her. This time, though, she was ready for it, throwing herself on the foaming crest, to be borne inshore by the force of the surging comber. She was dashed to her knees as the shining curl of green water splintered into white foam, then ebbed away. Again and again she returned to deeper water, her hair plastered behind her ears as she waited for a breaker to surge towards her and sweep her towards the shore.

The scene around her seemed to be bathed in liquid gold, the sun's rays throwing a glittering pathway over the sea. Everything else fled from her mind as she gave herself up to the enjoyment of sun and sea.

It was as she rounded the point at the end of the sheltered bay that she came in sight of a land-locked cove sealed on the seaward side by a rocky ledge. Her fascinated gaze swept the still water, and soon she was plunging into the sea, her clean strokes making scarcely a ripple on the green depths. Presently she pulled herself up on to the rocky ledge above, dropping down to seat herself on a boulder and then wringing out the long fall of streaming dark hair.

Her idle gaze went to the hills cut as sharply as cardboard shapes against the luminous blue of the sky, then her glance moved to the homestead. She could see no sign of life around the grounds, but over in the woolshed electric lights were burning.

Down here on the beach, though, she congratulated herself, she had the place to herself. Or could she be mistaken? she wondered the next moment. For along the vast stretch of sand a horseman was galloping towards her. Pray God it wasn't Jarrah Conway! Even as she made the silent plea, however, Liz recognised his athletic build and dark hair. He was bent low over his mount, she noticed, and all at once her taut nerves relaxed. No doubt he was engaged on a daily routine of exercising one of his horses along the beach before the intense heat of the day set in. He wouldn't be worrying about her. With a bit of luck he might not even notice her away out here above the cove. His horse's hoofs were pounding along the wet sand at the edge of the tide and advancing at such speed, she told herself hopefully, he would be past the cove without a sideways glance and around the point of the bay.

'Liz!' He had pulled his mount to a violent stop and was gazing in her direction. 'Come back!' His strong tones were carried towards her on the breeze and there was no mistaking the urgency of the gesture of his hands as he beckoned her towards him. 'You're asking for trouble out there!'

She sat motionless, regarding him with resentful eyes and tightly compressed lips. What was he on about, for heaven's sake? The rocky ledge above the land-locked cove was the last place in the world where one could imagine some lurking peril. If he had glimpsed her when she had been swimming far out at sea she would have understood his fears for her safety, for he would be unaware that she was an experienced swimmer. But out here on dry land—well, sharp rocks rather—really, it was quite ridiculous!

Cupping both hands around her mouth, she shouted

back a defiant 'No!' And to make her refusal to obey
orders perfectly clear to him, she lay back on her stony
perch. It was worth the acute discomfort she was
enduring to get through to him that she had no intention
of obeying his shouted commands. She didn't *have* to do
as the boss said. She wasn't on his payroll. After today
she would never set eyes on him again!

It was impossible, however, to remain unaware of his
continuous shouts that echoed across the water between
them. 'Step on it! Come back, Liz! I'm telling you, *come
back*!'

Despite the painful pressure of sharp rocks beneath
her Liz maintained her position and continued to ignore
his commanding tones.

What was the matter with the man? she thought in
exasperation. If he imagined he could order her around,
that he had merely to call and she would leap to obey . . .
The next moment, as if tuning in with her thoughts, a
piercing whistle echoed through the clear air. The
brute! He had put two fingers to his lips and whistled
her, just as if she were one of his sheepdogs.

Irritated now beyond words, she jumped to her feet
and waved both hands in a gesture of defiance. 'Go
away!' she called back angrily. 'Leave me alone!' She
stifled a momentary prick of conscience that she did
owe him something for his help with her car and his
hospitality.

Clearly, however, her refusal to do his bidding had no
effect whatever on him. He was dropping down from
the saddle and leading his mount towards a grassy strip
running down to meet the sand. The next moment she
realised that he was actually coming after her. Well, if
he chose to behave in so childish a fashion! Deliberately
Liz seated herself and turned her back towards him,
letting the sun dry the salt on her body.

Out of a corner of her eye, however, she was aware that he was advancing towards her, his muscular tanned legs taking him swiftly over the sharp rocky pile. She sneaked another glance and was forced to admit that with his thick dark hair blowing across his forehead and sunshine gleaming on bronzed shoulders and thighs, he looked attractive—very. He wore only swimming trunks and his bare sinewy chest glistening with drops of seawater told her that he had recently been swimming his horse in the surf. If only, she thought irritatedly, he would swim his mount right back across the bay and leave her alone! The way he was behaving towards her anyone would imagine she was in some sort of frightful danger out here, which was absurd!

He had all but reached her now, his tone sharp and accusing. 'What the hell do you think you're playing at?' Hadn't she sensed right from the beginning that he was one of that arrogant dictatorial breed of men? 'You little fool! Didn't you hear me yelling at you? Now come along, and make it quick!'

Lazily she turned to prop herself on an elbow, meeting his angry look with eyes sparkling with defiance. 'Why?'

'Because I'm telling you,' he gritted, 'that's why!' He had come to stand over her and his fierce expression was making her nervous. 'Come on! On your feet, girl!'

'I don't know,' she said, trying to keep her voice casual, 'what all the panic's about!'

'Are you coming with me,' his voice was dangerously quiet, 'or do I have to make you?'

'You couldn't—you wouldn't——'

'Try me!' There was something unnerving in his steely glance. He was standing motionless, glaring down at her. Like a wild animal, she thought, about to pounce on its prey.

'Anyway,' deliberately she lifted her small square chin and forced her voice to a light note, 'I'm staying right here, whether you like it or not!'

'Right!' Suddenly she was only too well aware that he meant business. Scrambling hurriedly to her feet, she took a step backwards, scarely conscious of a stab of pain on the ball of her foot cut by the razor-sharp edge of a seashell. Blood spurted from the wound, but neither of them were aware of it. Before she had time to argue the matter further he had picked her up in his arms and she found herself caught to his sinewy chest with its mat of wet black hair. 'Let me *go*!' She struggled wildly, kicking her legs and trying to loosen his hold, but it was useless. The steely strength she had suspected he possessed was now being demonstrated to her in no uncertain terms and the only effect of her exertions was to make him clasp her even more tightly, so close that she could feel the thud-thud of his heart.

'You're wasting your time!' he gritted. 'Nothing's going to hurt you, not if I can help it!'

Whatever he meant by that! Liz ceased her struggles against his confining arms that held her like steel bands. What was the use? He wasn't even breathing hard as he carried her—but of course, the thought ran through her mind, she meant no more to him than if he were carrying one of his sheep, only she happened to be a whole lot lighter in weight! She felt a hysterical desire to giggle. Instead she said coldly, her gaze on the sharp shell-encrusted rocks she had avoided with such care on her way out to the ledge, 'You'll cut your feet, the pace you're going!' For his bare brown feet were moving swiftly from rock to rock.

'That'll make two of us, won't it? It's not that danger that's on my mind!' Once again she was puzzled by his words. She gazed enquiringly up into his strong masculine face, and then it happened! A wild excitement was running along her nerves. Was it the warm closeness of his damp skin that was doing things to her, unexpected crazy things, like wanting to relax against his strong lithe body and just enjoy, enjoy . . . Or could it be his alive black-lashed hazel eyes that were meeting her glance full-on? Eyes so full of light and something else, unseen, potent, a life force running like electricity between them. Even after she had torn her gaze aside, the magic of the moment stayed with her. Just physical attraction, she told herself. Blame his male magnetism and the closeness of our bodies locked together. Two strangers in whom some force stronger than themselves had set a fire alight. To break the spell of her *awareness* of him as a man she forced her voice to a careless note and said mockingly, 'All this mad rush. I don't know what we're running away from.'

Jarrah Conway made no answer. Then as they reached the shore, he loosened his hold and unexpectedly, there it was again, the tingle of excitement shooting through her pulses as she slid down his sinewy body to the wet sand below. She glanced up at him and something in his expression of alertness, the way his eyes were gazing out to sea, made her follow his glance, then her eyes widened in horror and disbelief. 'It can't be,' she breathed, 'not out there! It looked so enclosed, so *safe*!' For even as she watched a towering wall of green came surging in from the sunlight-sparkled sea, faster, faster, to thunder against the rocky ledge, that innocent-looking ledge, in a welter of flying spray. It didn't take any special knowledge, Liz told herself in a rush of relief at her narrow escape, to know that anyone who had the misfortune to be trapped on the rocky ledge would have been swept away, helpless against the force of that swirling, turbulent sea.

She said very low, 'I never dreamed . . .' Looking up at him, she saw that his gaze was fixed on the water that was milling and tossing over the spot where she had been sunbathing only a few minutes earlier. She felt sick in her midriff. Where, had it not been for him . . . 'Sorry,' she whispered, 'if I'd known——' It was the best she could come up with in the way of an apology. She scarcely knew what she was saying, her thoughts were in such a turmoil, but Jarrah Conway seemed barely aware of her hesitant words.

'Folk who live around here avoid that ledge like the plague,' he was saying. 'Every once in a while a freak wave breaks over the rocks and there've been a heck of a lot of drownings out there, mostly fishermen who come in at the narrow entrance. To anyone who doesn't know the spot, it looks to be an ideal place to toss down your line in deep water. Actually it's got a reputation of being one of the most dangerous offshore fishing spots in the whole country!'

Liz sent him a swift glance. 'Why don't you put up a Danger notice there, then?'

'Good thinking! But how long do you think a board would last in those freak waves? Besides,' his searching glance was difficult to meet, 'would a Danger, Keep Out notice have stopped you from haring over there to take a look at the cove below, do you think?'

'I guess not,' she admitted ruefully.

All at once he became aware of the trickle of blood that was staining the sand below her foot. 'Give that a wash in seawater,' he said tersely, 'and see you don't get any sand in the wound afterwards or you could be in trouble. Out here we're miles away from a doctor where you could get a tetanus injection against infection!'

Liz let the next breaker wash over her foot, then she wrinkled her nose at him. 'I don't fancy hopping on one

foot all the way back to the homestead. And I can't see
what else I can do!'

'I can!' His lazy glance surveyed her, then to her
amazement, once again he gathered her in his arms and
carrying her as effortlessly as if she were a child, he
strode over the sand and made his way towards the
horse still grazing on the dried grass bordering the
beach. Liz was so astonished by his action that she lay
passive in his arms. In view of her earlier crashing
blunder regarding his intentions towards her, what
could she say? So she remained silent, despising herself
for the sense of ineffable relaxation that was stealing
over her senses. And just a short while ago she had been
about to marry Brooke, she chided herself. What
manner of girl was she? But of course the feelings that
being close to Jarrah evoked in her meant nothing.
They were born of reaction following a narrow escape
from death. Such an experience was bound to make her
feel a certain amount of warmth towards her rescuer,
even if he did happen to be the one man in the world she
wished to avoid.

Dreamily she was aware of the warmth of the sun on
her skin, of a blissful sensation of deep content laced
with stirrings of excitement. Not real content, of course,
merely relief after moments of danger. She wouldn't be
feeling this strange wild happiness in other circumstances, and especially not with Jarrah. It was just the
way things happened.

The cut on her foot left a trail of blood on the sand,
and when they reached the grazing horse, he tossed her
up on the horse's back, then freed the reins and jumped
up behind her. 'Ever ridden like this?' he asked.

'Lots of times!' What did he take her for, she
wondered indignantly, a city office worker? Aloud she
added, 'But I've usually gone riding on my own, not like

this!' *Not with your arms around me*!

Not with a man who affects me in this heart-stirring way, a small unwanted voice in her mind said. A stranger whose touch, nearness, voice, can do things to my peace of mind. But of course, she reasoned away the thought, it means nothing. It's Brooke I cared for. I must have cared for him to have wanted to marry him. Close on the reflection came another. How could I have been so crazy?

The horse's easy canter took them around the point of the bay and along the beach. They were in sight of the homestead when a rousing cheer echoed from a group of men who were advancing on horseback down the grassy slopes.

'Good for you, mate!'

'Reckon you'd qualify for mention as the Lifesaver of the Year Award after that little effort!'

'Now we know why he headed along the beach this morning!'

Jarrah responded to their raillery with a grin and a wave of the hand, then he slowed his mount to a trot and they took the winding path leading to the house. When they reached the verandah steps he dropped down to the path below. 'Wait here and don't put that foot to the ground till I get back!' he ordered.

'Right, boss!' Smiling mischievously, Liz sent him a smart salute. Dimples flickered in her cheeks. 'Just as you say, boss!' This time, she conceded, he did have some excuse for his peremptory tone of voice.

He was back almost at once, his long strides taking the steps two at a time. Then with deft movements of his fingers he placed a strip of bandage over the open wound. 'When you get inside,' he advised, 'bathe your foot in hot water. You'll find disinfectant in the medicine cabinet in the bathroom, that should give the healing some hurry-up.' He released her foot and she dropped to the ground.

'Thanks.' Why was it, she wondered, that she couldn't for long sustain his deep intent gaze? 'For everything,' she added in a rush of words. 'I guess if you hadn't come to my rescue——'

'All part of the service.' The deep smile lines flashed in his sun-bronzed face and once again it struck her how different he looked when he smiled. Younger, more carefree and more than ever disturbingly attractive, something deep inside her whispered.

He was turning away when she called to him. 'Oh, about Hercules—my car, when do you think it will be back here?'

His cool glance swept her face. 'You can't wait to get away from here, can you?'

And whose fault is that? Before Liz could speak the words that had sprung to her lips he was saying evenly, 'It should be back by midday. I've sent a man to fetch it and I'll have a word with Bill as soon as he gets the car in the garage.'

'I see.' There was just no getting the better of him, she mused.

She watched him ride away, horse and rider silhouetted against the bright sunshine. It seemed incredible, she reflected as she limped towards her bedroom, that it was still early in the day.

Back in her room she paused, arrested by her reflection in the bureau mirror. Considering her recent escape from death out on the ledge she would have expected herself to appear a complete wreck. On the contrary, she looked—well, different; misty-eyed, with softly flushed cheeks. It must be the effect of sea and sun, she decided, that made her look almost as if she were—a girl in love!

After a breakfast that consisted of stewed white peaches from the orchard, followed by coffee, toast and marmalade, Liz made her way out to the jasmine-scented verandah and stood looking over the railing. There seemed no limit to this property of Jarrah's she mused, her gaze sweeping the vista of hills with bush-filled gullies dividing the paddocks and forming natural boundaries. Her gaze went to the sandy track leading down the hillside. Before long Hercules would be coming down the slope, albeit in tow, bound for the garages below and the attentions of a skilled mechanic.

'Looking for a job, Liz?' Mrs Malloy had appeared in the open doorway and was setting down a cane basket and a huge woven flax kit. 'How about taking morning smoko over to the woolshed for me? You'll just make it in time if you go now.'

'Love to.' Liz moved to take the basket with its packed sandwiches and crusty scones still hot from the oven. In the other hand she grasped the Maori kit with mugs, milk, tea, sugar and a massive aluminium teapot.

Presently she was passing an enclosure where sheep were penned, then she climbed the old kauri steps of the big timber shed. Inside the iron-roofed building she was met by a blast of hot air, and as she moved into the heat and dust and activity of the shed the noise of the machines was deafening and the smell of sheep overpowering.

Putting down her baskets, she stood silently watching the ceaseless activity that was going on around her. In the stands shearers bent low over the animals held firmly in their grasp, the men's muscles rippling in powerful shoulders as with speed and precision they sheared away the heavy fleece. A 'rousie' was filling a pen and a 'fleeco', a man wielding a broom, was clearing away bits and pieces of wool from the oil-slippery floor.

'Smoko!' As the loud cry echoed through the high-rafted building, machines were switched off and everything was quiet. The last remaining sheep was pushed down the chute where, as if in sheer enjoyment of its freedom, it skipped away on the grass to rejoin its companions.

In the sudden stillness shearers straightened muscular bodies gleaming with sweat and wiped their hands and faces with their handkerchiefs. They moved towards the bench were Liz filled the mugs from the giant-sized teapot. 'Milk, everyone?' she asked.

'You bet!' came a chorus of male voices.

Around her the masculine talk eddied as thirsty men gulped down the hot tea and soon she was busy refilling the mugs.

'Looks like you're not new to all this,' one of the men commented as he held out his mug.

'That's right,' she sent him a smile, 'I'm a country girl myself.'

'Good for you!' His appreciative glance rested on her tanned young face. 'We all feel the same way. It takes guts to join in this sort of game, but it's worth it! Good team-mates, a change of scenery every few weeks and now and again,' he grinned, 'we strike a bonus—like you!'

Suddenly the smoko break was over and the men returned to their tasks. The rousie was bringing in sheep from the pen outside, machines were switched on and the frenzied activity of the shed swung back into action.

Liz packed mugs and containers back into the basket and flax kit. She hadn't expected there would be any food left over. Then she went out into the sunlight once again. As she made her way along the narrow track she hurried towards the garages where a man was bending over the open bonnet of her car. 'It's Bill, isn't it?' she said as she limped towards him. 'I'm Liz, the owner of that funny-looking old car that let me down on the road yesterday.'

He slammed down the bonnet of the vehicle and turned to face her, wiping grease-stained hands on an oil rag. A middle-aged man, he had a slow manner of speaking and a clear honest gaze. 'Hi, Liz, I guessed who you were. You want a verdict on the trouble? Well, I've given your old bus the once-over and she's in fairly good nick. All that's wrong——'

'The battery!' she broke in. 'It's flat, isn't it? The shearers thought——'

'They were dead right! All you need is a new one and you'll be away laughing, back on the road in no time. Bad luck that I haven't got a spare in stock right now. Most times we keep one or two on hand.'

'Oh!' Liz's face fell. 'Will that mean,' she said slowly, 'that someone will have to pick one up from the nearest town?'

'That's about it.'

'Will there be anyone from Hauturu going into town soon, do you think?' She tried to hide the note of anxiety in her voice. 'Today, maybe?'

He shook his head regretfully. 'Not that I know of.'

'How about a special trip, then?' She smiled engagingly up into his kindly face. 'Tell me, Bill, what do you think of my chances?'

He rubbed his chin doubtfully. 'That would be up to the boss. You'll have to have a word with Jarrah on that one. Around here he's the one who calls the shots.'

'Don't I know it!' she groaned.

'He won't see you stuck,' the friendly tones went on. Jarrah! Liz wasn't so sure on that point. Fat chance of her being able to talk the boss into granting any special favours on her behalf!

'Why don't you go and see him—he's down in the yards,' suggested Bill.

'Why not?' She flashed him a smile over her shoulder. 'Thanks for getting the car back here, Bill.'

'Good luck!'

'I'll need it.' She tried to cheer her drooping spirits as she moved away. The boss isn't all that anxious to have me around, she thought. He might stretch a point and send someone to make a special trip. Well, he might. All at once she couldn't wait to put it to him.

CHAPTER THREE

WHEN she reached the yards, however, it was a young stockman who approached her through a cloud of rising dust. 'Jarrah?' he said in answer to her enquiry. 'You've just missed him. He left here to see to the pump down in the gully.' He sent her a shy grin. 'If I can be of any help, just say the word——'

'Afraid not,' Liz said on a sigh. Then all at once a thought struck her and she smiled up into the open boyish face. 'Maybe there is something you could help me with. How about finding me a horse to ride?' She tried to disguise the note of urgency in her tones. 'I just felt like a ride, it's that sort of a day, and I may as well find the boss and have a word with him about my car.'

He pushed his wide-brimmed hat to the back of his head, leaving a red line across his forehead. 'You can take my mare Katie. She's tied up over there in the corral.' Together they strolled towards the heavily-built grey mare standing quietly in the shade of the macrocarpas. 'She's not the world's fastest racer, but you won't have to bail out in a hurry—— Wait there and I'll get you a saddle.'

'There's no need!' Already Liz was freeing the mount and slipping the bridle over the mare's head. The young stockman helped her up on to the mare's broad back.

'Take the bridle track behind the homestead,' he advised her, 'over the next hill and down the slope and you'll hit the gully.'

'Thanks a lot—what was your name?'

'Gary.' A wide grin lighted his tanned features.

'Well, thanks again, Gary.'

'Any time.' He stood watching her as she rode away.

Soon she was urging her mount to an easy canter, her dark hair streaming in a cloud behind her ears as the mare took a sheep track winding over sun-dried slopes. The stockhorse, evidently accustomed to the route, wheeled and waited while her rider opened and closed farm gates.

Presently, as she took a downward slope, Liz caught a glimpse of a horse grazing in the shade of lacy-fronded ponga trees that crowded the gully below. The next moment, finding her way barred by a great fallen tree, she pressed her knees against against the mare's warm flanks and set her mount to the jump. Katie responded by gathering herself to sail effortlessly over the barrier to land safely further down the incline.

Liz leaned forward to give the mare an appreciative pat, then horse and rider went on down the hillside. Presently the echo of running water was in her ears and reaching the thickly growing native bush with its damp earthy fragrance, she left the mare to graze on the fresh grass bordering the stream while she advanced on foot.

She saw Jarrah almost at once. He was standing in the crystal-clear water clearing the inlet of the pump, and Liz, moving silently on the damp leafmould underfoot, took a sneaky delight in surprising him. 'Hey there!' she called.

He swung around to face her, tossing the thatch of thick black hair from his tanned forehead. His expression, she realised frustratedly, was more wary then startled. 'Go on, say it!' The words burst from her lips before she could stop them. 'Not *you* again!'

His glance was inscrutable as he waded through the running water to drop down on the grassy bank in the filtered sunshine.

'Take a seat,' he invited, and Liz flung herself down at his side.

His next words were the last ones she would have expected to hear from him. No apology for his verbal attack on her last night, not even a polite 'What brings you here, Liz?' No hint of curiosity at her unexpected arrival in the gully. Oh no, nothing like that! Merely a disapproving glance towards her bandaged foot and a sharply spoken enquiry, 'You're keeping that wound clean, aren't you? There's no throbbing around the area of the cut? No sign of inflammation around it?'

At his staccato tones her eyes twinkled mischievously. 'Yes, sir! No, sir! Permission to present foot for inspection—sir!' Kicking off her rubber sandal, she stretched out a suntanned foot.

'Let me see!' He bent over her, a bronzed well-shaped hand encircling her slim ankle. Then it happened all over again—a tingle of excitement running through her nerves. She was totally unprepared for the reaction his touch on her skin evoked. The thought ran through her mind that she was indeed aware of a throbbing sensation. It was pulsing through her veins like wildlife. Fighting against the tumult of her senses, she jerked herself free and rushed into speech. 'That wasn't the reason I came here to see you——'

'No?' came the lazy vibrant tones. His sideways glance, deep and intent, said a lot more, things that right at this moment Liz wasn't prepared to face up to. His glinting hazel eyes mocked her. 'You couldn't resist the opportunity, admit it?'

'*No!*' Instinctively the vehement denial burst from her lips. The next minute a shattering suspicion struck her, suppose his words hadn't been joke-talk, that he actually believed her to have followed him to this lonely spot where they could be alone together? Knowing the opinion he had formed of her ... She could feel the humiliating tide of colour rushing up her cheeks and hurriedly she averted her face. What was he thinking? The answer came unbidden. The worst, of course, what else?

'That had nothing to do with it,' she protested in confusion, and realised the next minute that her stupid phrasing of the words had only served to make matters worse. She gathered her senses together and tried for composure. 'I just had to see you about something important,' she said, and rushed on in a flurry of words before he could make something of that. 'It's about Hercules——'

'Oh, your car?' She dropped her gaze before his disconcerting look. 'Why didn't you say so?'

Restlessly she plucked at a piece of grass. 'You knew it would be about that,' she said very low. Unfortunately her next words betrayed her. 'What else could it be?'

'Ask yourself!' Jarrah's mocking drawl sent her thoughts spinning in confusion. She drew a deep breath. 'The thing is,' she ran on, determined not to allow herself to be sidetracked once again by his suspicion of her motives—*or bewitched by the magic of his deep tones* an unwanted voice deep in her mind said.

She thrust it aside and hurried on. 'I've seen Bill and he's had a look at my car and it's just as the shearing gang told me yesterday, the battery's had it—absolutely!' She tried for lightness. 'Seems that all I need to get myself mobile again is a brand new battery for Hercules.' She sent him a glance which she hoped was confident and carefree, but there was a betraying wobble in her voice. 'Now it all depends on you!'

'On me?' Jarrah was lying back on the grass, arms crossed behind his head, regarding her lazily. His thickly marked eyebrows rose and he enquired with deceptive innocence, 'What have I got to do with it?'

Liz sighed exasperatedly. He was being deliberately obtuse. With an effort she forced back the angry retort

his bantering attitude had goaded her into. Why must
she keep forgetting, she reminded herself grimly, that
only this morning he had saved her life?

'Oh, you know what I mean,' she muttered resentfully.

He made no answer but continued to regard her with
his bland enquiring stare, and all at once she forgot all
about being grateful to him for his timely rescue earlier
in the day and the advantages of using a certain degree
of tact in view of her present dependent circumstances.

'Do I have to spell it out?' she blurted out crossly. 'I
can't possibly get away from here until the car has a new
battery, and Bill says he doesn't know of anyone from
the station who plans on going to a town this week. He
told me to have a word with you about it—so here I am!
Not,' she added bitterly, 'that it's doing me the least bit
of good!'

Once again she became aware of the sardonic gleam
in his eyes. 'You don't seem at all humble about it,' he
observed.

Goaded beyond endurance, Liz glared at him.
'Should I be?'

'No—but it helps.'

His eyes held an expression she couldn't interpret.
'You mean you're going to help me out?' she urged.
'You'll send someone into town to pick up a new battery
for Hercules?'

'Sure,' he murmured in his maddening drawl, his eyes
half-closed against the sun-glare. 'Not this week,
though—or the next!'

Anger mushroomed in her like a black cloud. The
brute, she thought hotly, the cruel sadistic brute! He
had led her on to imagine he was on her side and
now—— She said very low, 'I might have known you
wouldn't do a thing to help me. Just because . . .' Her
words trailed away into silence, for meeting his glance

she saw there was no lightness in his look. The hazel eyes were steely and so was his tone.

'Did you really expect me to take a man from his duties here at a busy time of the year just so that you could get on with what you want to do, taking pretty photographs of the scenery,' suddenly his merciless gaze raked her, 'or is it men friends you're collecting on the trip?'

'Oh——' a rose flush stained her cheeks, 'if it's Greg you're getting at——'

He shrugged away her angry protests. 'What does it matter who he is? It's none of my business!'

'No, it's not!'

His well-shaped lips twisted in a sardonic smile. 'At least you agree with me on one thing!'

'Oh,' Liz made a despairing gesture with her hand, 'what's the use of trying to explain anything to you!' she cried in angry frustration, 'you'd never believe a word I said anyway!'

Her thoughts were in a tumult and she tried to rationalise away the frustration that consumed her. Does his opinion of my motives really matter, seeing I'll be here so brief a time? she thought. And yet in some odd hurtful way, it did. It mattered a lot. She pulled her thoughts back to his contained tones.

'Like I said, you're welcome to stay——'

'You keep telling me that!' she broke in fiercely. She might just have well not have spoken, however, for all the notice he took of her.

'For as long as you wish.'

'You mean,' she snapped at him, 'for as long as *you* wish!'

Jarrah simply ignored the remark. 'Give it a week or two and things will have sorted themselves out. Then I'll see what I can do for you.'

Liz was too incensed to choose her words. 'If you

expect me to get down on my knees in gratitude for
that——'

'Tell me something,' she was aware that he was
regarding her narrowly, 'just why are you in such a
hurry to get away from here? You've got no bookings
ahead and plenty of time to roam around the country
and please yourself, so what's the rush?'

'You—you——' Liz was all but choking with indignation. 'Do you think,' she demanded hotly, 'that I want
to stay here of all places after the things you said to me
last night, *untrue* things that Brooke told you about me!'

His mouth was a grim line. 'I've only got your word
for that!'

'You're so sure of yourself,' she protested, 'believing
lies about me just because you happen to be related to
Brooke—well, sort of. If you knew me better——'

'If that's all that's troubling you——' The hazel eyes
mocked her. Before she could guess his intention he had
leaned over and in a swift movement he gathered her to
him, so close she could feel through his thin cotton shirt
the warmth of his sinewy chest pressed close to her soft
body. For a timeless moment he looked deep into her
eyes, and at something in his expression the fragrant
green world around them slipped away and a wild
excitement pulsed through her veins.

Deep down something urged her to wrench herself
free of his strong confining arms, but another part of her
mind urged her to submit to his hard-muscled strength.
The seductive voice in her mind won a victory and she
relaxed against him. The next moment his mouth came
down on hers in a hard punishing kiss, and when at last
she struggled free of his detaining arms, her hand flew
to her mouth as if to wipe away the memory of his
merciless caress. Dazed and trembling, she sprang to
her feet, the thought spinning through her mind that
Jarrah's sun-hardened features wore an oddly unfami-

liar expression, almost as though he too had been
unexpectedly shaken by the incident. But that, she told
herself the next moment, was plainly absurd, for now he
was regarding her with a look of indolent amusement.

It came to her then that she should have taken heed of
the part of her mind that had warned her to make her
escape from Jarrah's embrace. There was danger in
being held close in his arms.

One kiss, she mocked her runaway thoughts, and a
hard punitive kiss at that! What's in a kiss? Nevertheless ... Without a word she turned away and moved
towards the grazing mare. Taking a firm hold on the
flowing mane, she pulled herself up on the sun-warmed
grey back and gathered the reins in her hands. All the
time she was aware of Jarrah. He was lying back on the
grass once again, his eyes veiled watching her ... just
watching.

At last she pulled on the rein and faced him,
conscious all over again of his deep unfathomable look.

'Running away, Liz?' came the drawling tones.

Bright danger flags flew in her cheeks and just in time
she recalled the purpose of his visit. Deliberately she
misconstrued his query. 'No such luck!' The bemuse-
ment of his touch fell away to be replaced by spirited
challenge. 'How could I possibly do that,' she summoned a cheeky smile, 'without your help?'

On horseback, freed of the crazy excitement of his
touch, it was easier, she found, to get herself back to her
old defensive attitude towards him. She sat still waiting
for him to tell her that of course he would see about
getting her back on the road. That he had intended all
along to send a man to town to get a battery for her car.
He had only been mocking her when he had told her
that she would have to wait for two long weeks here in
his home, dependent on his reluctant hospitality. For
even though the kiss that had shaken her world hadn't

meant a great deal to him, she told herself, it surely must have meant *something*! Apparently not, she decided the next minute as Jarrah said nothing but merely went on regarding her with his amused, speculative gaze.

Nettled, she heard herself saying the first words that sprang into her mind. 'I wouldn't mind having to wait here and all that if I had a job, something to do.'

All at once his lazy glance was bright and alert. 'Earn your keep, you mean? If that's what what you want, why not?'

At the kindling of interest in his eyes Liz knew a moment's panic. What work was he planning to offer her? she wondered uneasily. No doubt he had in mind some demanding physical task that no one else in his employ wanted to take on. Looking down at him, she said carefully, 'What did you have in mind?'

He said carelessly, 'You can take over training the horses if you want something to do and don't mind getting up at the crack of dawn to take a run along the beach every day.'

'I don't mind.' Anything to show him that she had no intention of being indebted to him for his hospitality! She brought her mind back to the resonant tones.

'Come and see me in the office after dinner tonight and I'll give you a run-down on the programme.'

She schooled her voice to a careless note, determined to give the lie to her betraying response to the traitorous delight of his kiss. 'What makes you think I can ride well enough to train your horses?' she asked. 'I mean, Katie doesn't count for much. She's built like a tank.'

'Maybe. But taking her over that jump on the side of the hill is something else again. A good effort,' he acknowledged.

'You saw me coming!' she accused, trying to hide the ridiculous rush of pleasure his compliment had brought her.

He grinned maddeningly. 'Anything wrong with that?'

'Of course not.' But beneath the conventional words her thoughts were rioting. So he had known of her approach all along. Her arrival in the gully had been no surprise to him at all. No doubt he had been expecting her to come to him begging for help with her car. She must have been out of her mind, she told herself bitterly, to have expected him to do anything constructive about her difficulties.

His drawling tones cut across her thoughts. 'You're a show-jumper, aren't you?'

She nodded. 'I've attended shows all over the country,' she acknowledged, and held her breath for his next question. It came.

'With Brooke?'

Unconsciously Liz's hands tightened nervously on the reins. 'Sometimes. I'd better get back to the house. 'Bye now.'

Jarrah lifted his hand in a gesture of farewell, making no attempt to detain her. Liz dug her heels into the mare's broad flanks and rode away. Halfway up the green slope she pulled her mount to a halt and glanced back towards the gully below, to catch a glimpse of Jarrah working once more in the stream as he cleared the choked inlet to the pump.

Just a temporary interruption to his labours, she told herself, that was all the interlude had meant to him! It made her feel angry all over again just thinking about him.

Liz found a perverse satisfaction in the knowledge that Jarrah did not arrive back at the homestead for the evening meal until long after everyone else had left the table. Serve him right if he had had difficulty in fixing the pump in the gully to his satisfaction! Chances were

he would have forgotten all about his promise to find
her some riding employment while she was here.
Thinking of him from a business angle, she found, was
easier than from a personal one. That way madness lay.
Didn't she know it!

That evening she wandered restlessly around her
room, staring aimlessly out of the window at the
darkening scene outside. She was postponing the
interview with the boss, why not admit it? But there was
something about him that was unnerving, a sensation
that was new to her.

She hadn't imagined that any man could cause her to
feel this way, uncertain and tremulous and vulnerable.
But then never before had she found herself stranded in
the outback and forced to be dependent on the reluctant
hospitality of a stranger.

Jarrah's high-handed attitude towards her did nothing to ease the disconcerting position in which she
found herself. If only I'd known, she vowed silently,
that he was going to enjoy himself so much in putting
me down today I would never have handed him the
opportunity. I wouldn't have allowed him to kiss me
either!

But deep down where it counted she knew she had
been swept by forces beyond her control. Never again!
Now that she knew the effect his touch could have on
her stupid senses she would be prepared. Feeling mad
with him, she found, helped to chase away the
traitorous emotions that thoughts of his caress evoked.

Right now while she was still hating him, she cheered
herself, would be a good time to face the boss in his
office. But if he imagines I'm going to beg for his
favours, she set her lips firmly, he's way out of line!

Squaring her shoulders and lifting her small rounded
chin, she marched resolutely up the long carpeted hall.
A light gleamed from beneath the door of the office and

Liz pushed open the door and went inside to find the room empty, no matter, she could wait.

She approached the wide desk with its litter of wages sheets, files, account books and correspondence, then her gaze lifted to the wall above, with its huge aerial map of the property. Swiftly she took in the contours with the boundaries of Maori land and scenic views of the vast station holding.

Presently her roving glance went to the opposite wall and a framed picture of a young woman. Red-haired with sleepy eyes and a provocative smile, the girl had a sort of off-beat beauty. There was something about her, something that was attention-getting, arresting, different. The type of person who would command instant attention wherever she went, and with whom many man would fall in love. Liz took in the scrawled signature across the corner of the photograph. 'To Jarrah with love—Bridget.' Was he in love with her? Now where could that thought have come from? she asked herself. As if she cared about his love-life.

Liz shifted her attention to the various newspaper clippings and photographs taken at horse trials and agricultural shows, and shots of prize-winning animals. A massive woolly ram stared belligerently at her from a backdrop of a country saleyard.

Curiously she moved on, standing on tiptoe to view pictures of international racing car circuits. A photograph taken at a Monaco circuit held her interest. 'Jarrah Conway, Grand Prix winner.' The newspaper clipping showed him facing an array of silver cups, a champagne bottle fizzing in his hand.

'Interested in racing cars, are you?'

She spun around to find him standing motionless in the doorway regarding her with those disturbing eyes of his.

'Yes, well—I don't know much about it really. But

this picture looks interesting.' Her lips twitched at the corners. 'I see that you're getting into the bubbly!'

'Just one of the perks of the game!'

'If you're a winner!' It was a relief to her that he apparently was going to make no mention of the incident in the gully today. Maybe he had already forgotten. Well, that was fine with her.

'This caption intrigues me.' Liz had moved on to scan another newspaper photograph, reading the heading aloud. 'A sight that would be unthinkable in Europe— Jarrah Conway, the most experienced driver around the Pukekohe circuit, helping out a fellow competitor about to check the timing on his Chevron N39.'

He had come to stand at her side, so close she caught the tangy fragrance of after-shave lotion. Freshly showered, wearing a white cotton-knit shirt and immaculately tailored fawn slacks, he looked, she admitted reluctantly, wildly attractive—and more indomitable than ever! Swiftly she gathered her thoughts together. 'I can see you——' she broke off, amending 'are' for the 'have been' that trembled on her lips, 'experienced in all this.'

Jarrah seemed not to notice her moment of hesitation. 'I had a heck of a lot of fun in the game, enjoyed the travel, the excitement and the sheer thrill of racing,' his gaze went to the last photograph on the wall, with a crashed car and an unconscious driver spreadeagled on the circuit, '*while it lasted.*'

Lost in thoughts of the past, he seemed to have forgotten her presence. 'Funny that, you kid yourself that you've forgotten all about that other life, put it out of your mind and then something happens and pow! it's all back again! With me it happens every time I go back to Pukekohe——' His thoughtful gaze was still on the pictures of racing cars and he appeared to have forgotten who it was he was talking to. 'Ever been to Pukekohe, Liz?'

She shook her head. 'No, but I know of it. Isn't that the town where the New Zealand Grand Prix is held each January?'

'That's it.' She followed his glance to a newspaper picture of a racing car speeding down the circuit against a backdrop of thousands of onlookers. The printed headline leaped to her gaze: 'Jarrah Conway leads the pack off the startline in Saturday's International Grand Prix.'

There was a veiled expression in his eyes. 'It's a sleepy little town that comes to life on one day of the year, the day of the Grand Prix,' he told her.

'And you go back then to take a look at the races?'

'I was there last year and it sure got to me—the roar of the engines, the smell of the oil! I was right there, living it all over again, and then——'

'And then?'

He shrugged broad shoulders. 'Once I got back home I forgot all about it. Nowadays this is what counts in my scheme of things. Being right here in Hauturu!' His glance swept the aerial map depicting the old kauri homestead facing the sea, the rolling hills and far-flung boundaries of the vast property. All at once his deep tones rang with enthusiasm. 'This is where I belong, right here.'

For something to say Liz enquired, 'Have your folks always lived at Hauturu?'

He nodded. 'My grandfather started it all, came out by sailing ship from Scotland and bought a tract of land from the Maoris. In those early days it was virgin bush and a pretty tough proposition to tame. Later on my father put in a lifetime of hard work breaking in the land. For him it was nothing but backbreaking slog, day in and day out.'

'Tough for him.'

'Sure was, with no access to the outside world then except by sea, so the wool bales were taken away from Hauturu by boat. Me, I'm lucky enough to have the chance of developing land with the help of scientific know-how plus farm machinery and helicopters for spraying and all the help in the world——' He bent on her his deep intent gaze. 'Am I boring you?'

'No, no, you're not!' And strangely enough it was the truth.

'Up in that area of heavy bush, for instance.' He indicated a green patch on the map, leaning so close that Liz could feel his breath stirring the hair on her forehead, and fool that she was she was aware of his nearness in every fibre of her being. Through the confusion of her senses she struggled to concentrate on his words. 'Since that shot was taken all the bush has been burned off, stumps of trees cleared away and cropdusters brought in to fly over the hills and scatter fertiliser over barren slopes. Nowadays those hills are planted in young pines, seedlings that will be fully developed in a few years' time. I'll take you up there to have a look at the plantation one day if you like?'

'Oh, I would!' Strange, she mused, how normal her voice sounded. Jarrah was moving away from her, approaching his desk, and at last she was able to fight her way out of the seductive sweetness that was taking over her senses. How did it happen that tonight Jarrah seemed to her to be an entirely different man from their previous acquaintance? But only because, she decided ruefully, he's forgotten all about who I *really* am. To him right now I'm nothing but an audience, someone he can talk to about his plans and hopes for the future of his property. In a way it was a relief that apparently to him the romantic interlude of the afternoon had been no more than a passing impulse, already forgotten. It was what she wanted, wasn't it? So why feel this odd sense of let-down?

'These days,' he was saying, 'I'm more interested in racing horses than cars.' Dropping down to the big revolving chair, he motioned Liz to a seat opposite him at the desk.

Getting their relationship down to that of employer and employee, she reflected as she seated herself, would make the situation between them easier to handle. At least on that footing she knew where she stood with him.

'Ever done any racehorse training?'

His query took her by surprise and she knew that under the impact of those lively hazel eyes she would stand no chance at all of evading the truth. 'A little,' she was choosing her words carefully, 'but it was a while ago. Last summer, actually.' Last summer ... Her thoughts slipped back to the long summer holidays a year ago. Her father at that time had been in his usual excellent health and was happily absorbed in training the thoroughbred horse he had bred and broken in and used on the farm. She could still hear her father's happy tones: 'Mate's got a lot of promise, Liz. Look at his action!'

Her own voice, happy, excited. 'Just what I've been thinking! Imagine, one day he could make a name for himself on the race track!' She had turned to him impulsively. 'Dad, why don't you let me take a share of the schooling——'

'If that's what you want.' His eyes twinkled. 'Why d'you think I named him Liz's Mate?'

To Liz it had come as a bitter blow to learn, soon after she had returned to teaching at a school many miles distant, that a tractor accident had forced her father to give up training the big chestnut gelding for which they had both held such high hopes. She had been distressed and disappointed when the horse had been sold.

All at once she became aware of Jarrah's assessing
gaze. Then suddenly his expression lightened and
strong white teeth flashed against the bronze of his face.
'You're my girl!' he exclaimed exultantly. 'You're just
what I've been looking for!'

His heart-knocking grin, the way in which he was
regarding her as if he had just discovered not only the
end of the rainbow but the pot of gold as well, was doing
things to her composure, sending her thoughts spinning
in confusion. She pulled her mind back to his voice.
Trying to collect her scattered wits. What was he
saying? something about running beach races here once
a year? What could be the matter with her tonight, to
imagine crazy things like Jarrah caring about her in
some very special sort of way?

Careful, girl, she chided herself. You made a dreadful
mistake falling in love with Brooke almost at sight and
look where that foolishness led you! You can't afford to
make the blunder all over again with even more
disastrous results. *Especially not with Jarrah, of all men*!

'Put it this way,' came the deep tones, 'I've got a job
lined up for you.' Aware of his quizzical gaze, Liz
writhed inwardly in humiliation. Damn him, he seemed
to possess a power of reading her mind, of knowing that
she had misinterpreted the sudden light of appreciation
and pleasure in his eyes as he surveyed her small,
slender body. He more than suspected that she had read
an entirely mistaken significance into the warmth of his
tone. For herself, she jerked herself upright in the chair,
she was only too relieved to find that his attitude
towards her was quite impersonal. *That's because it's the
only way you can keep your runaway emotions in check*! a
small unwanted voice whispered deep in her mind. She
thrust it aside and said brightly, 'On the way here I
noticed a signpost advertising beach races.' It was

amazing, another part of her mind registered, how normal her voice sounded. She turned her attention back to his level tones.

'Years ago when my dad was running the outfit, horse races along the beach were an annual event along this coast, then later on he gave away the idea. I'm bringing it back, starting as from now! You could say,' once again Jarrah flashed her that devastating smile, 'that I happen to have racing blood in my veins! And that,' leaning back in his seat, he regarded her with gloating satisfaction—there was no other word for it, she thought, 'is where you come into the picture.'

'As a rider, you mean?'

'That's the idea. Now you——' He stopped short, taking in her mutinous expression. 'What's wrong? I thought you were looking for work?'

'I am. It's just—— You might have asked me if I'd agree to help you out!' Liz burst out indignantly. 'You make it sound like—like an order! As if you only have to snap your fingers and I'll jump to it!'

'So that's it!' His mouth was a thin, taunting line. 'Okay, if that's what's bugging you——' There was a mocking glint in the hazel eyes. 'How about it, Liz? I'm offering you a job training my thoroughbred. Same rates of pay as my other trainer was getting with the usual hours of work. I'll give you your instructions later.'

'You sound awfully keen to get someone to ride your horse!'

'That's right,' he agreed smoothly, 'just like you're keen to get a job. Now that we've got that wrapped up——'

'There you go again!' Liz was determined to hold her end up and to repay him for the accusations he had flung at her last night.

'For Pete's sake,' his low angry tone told her that she

had provoked the reaction she had hoped for, 'do you want the job or don't you?'

'I want it.'

'Great.' The relief in his tones confirmed her suspicions of how much he needed her for this particular work. All at once he was relaxed and happy. 'Fate's on my side,' he grinned, 'seeing that I've scheduled the beach races for the low tide in three weeks' time—— You'll be around?' Beneath the conventional words she caught a sharp note of interrogation. 'You can stay that long?'

'I have no choice in the matter,' she said huffily, 'and you know it!'

'Lucky for me!' Swiftly he brushed aside her resentful comment. 'Now this,' he ran on with enthusiasm, 'is what I want you to do.'

Liz pressed her lips firmly together. It was his attitude that riled her. Arrogant, autocratic, downright bossy! She wrenched her mind back to his deep tones.

'I've got a horse I picked up at the yearling sales a while ago. A gelding, nice manners, well bred. He's been broken in, and like the guy who bred him I happen to have a lot of faith in him. I reckon he's got a promising future ahead of him on the racetrack. He wouldn't be the first farm-trained horse to finish up winning the Melbourne Cup! I've been working at getting him fit and that's one reason I'm putting him into the beach races. If he does well there I'll enter him for meetings all over the country.'

His sun-darkened face was alight with enthusiasm. 'Your job will be to take him around the track a few times a day, give him a practice along the road, ride him down to the beach and give him a gallop along the sand. The man I had training him went off in a hurry when he was offered a job on a stud farm that his brother runs up north. Got the idea?'

Liz eyed him, her eyes wide and puzzled. 'What makes you so sure that I can handle the training of your thoroughbred? I mean to say, you and I, we——'

'Scarcely know each other? Is that it?' Tilting back his chair, Jarrah regarded her with a veiled expression in his eyes.

She could feel the pink creeping up her cheeks and she refused to meet his mocking glance. She just knew it would be mocking! He would take the opportunity of reminding her of that brief madness down by the stream in the valley. The next moment she realised to her relief that his tone was entirely matter-of-fact.

'I can size up an experienced rider when I see one, and in my book you happen to have that special something that's the important thing where I'm concerned.' All at once his tones rang with enthusiasm. 'You're just what I've been looking for! I'd just about given up hope of dropping on to anyone who could fill my special requirements, and now——'

'Me?' She looked at him in bewilderment. Could he be telling her that she possessed some specially appealing quality that she hadn't guessed at? That triumphant note in his voice a few moments ago . . . Did he really mean—— 'You're my girl!' Her thoughts were rioting in such wild confusion it was difficult to school her voice to a light, uncaring note. 'I can't think what you're getting at!'

'Can't you?' His appraising glance flickered over her and she was very much aware that he was giving her the once-over. 'Shall I let you into it, then? Thing is, I can't find a rider anywhere around here who would be light enough to take my horse along the sand in the beach races, and then—you come along!' Once again his appreciative glance slid over her. 'Just made for my purpose!'

Wildly Liz searched her mind for a put-down that

would prick his obvious smug satisfaction in having found her—*found her*! But all she could come up with was: 'I didn't come along especially to help you out in a horse race. It's just,' she tried to make her tone cutting, 'that I haven't any say in things here. I keep telling you!'

'I've shanghaied you into it, you mean?' Her lips tightened at the glint of amusement in his eyes. 'What's the odds, when I've got my jockey all ready-made?'

Breathless with indignation, she tried to think up a sufficiently cutting retort, but it was no use, her brain refused to function. 'Okay,' she said shortly, 'when do you want me to get started on this training programme of yours?'

'Now you're talking!' Completely ignoring her discouraging tone of voice, Jarrah swept on, 'Just as soon as you like. How about tomorrow, early? I'll have the horse ready in the stables and meet you there at five.' All at once his tones were threaded with urgency. 'You won't let me down?'

'Why should I?' Could he be getting at her because of his mistaken ideas concerning herself and his stepbrother? But no, his concern appeared to be only for his own interests. It came to her in that moment that the matter of her training his thoroughbred mattered to him a whole lot more than he was letting on.

'It's terribly important to you, all this, isn't it?' Before he could make an answer she pressed home her advantage. 'I guess,' she said mockingly, 'that even the big boss can't magic a lightweight rider out of the air at a moment's notice. Especially someone who has the know-how.'

'You've got something there,' Jarrah conceded, his even tones giving nothing away.

Liz's recently deflated spirits were rising with a rush. He's actually dependent on me when it comes to this horse training of his! she thought. In view of all she had been through at his hands the realisation was so breathtaking that it went to her head and she couldn't help the quirky smile that lifted the corners of her lips.

'What's so funny?' he demanded softly. Oh, she might have known he wouldn't miss her sudden change of expression.

'Nothing really.' She got to her feet and faced him. 'Just a silly thought that crossed my mind! I mean, I was so dependent on you for transport and somewhere to stay and all, and now,' there was something disconcerting in his gaze and she hurried on in a rush of words, 'all of a sudden it's the other way around and *you* have to rely on *me*!'

Jarrah rose from his seat, and she felt very small as he towered above her, an inscrutable expression in his eyes.

'Jockeywise, that is,' she amended hastily. 'Meet you at the stables in the morning,' she added breathlessly, and turned towards the door.

And for that appointment, she vowed silently, come hell or high water, she wouldn't be one minute late!

CHAPTER FOUR

THROUGH the hours of darkness Liz tossed and turned, waking and dozing off again, and when finally she opened her eyes it was to find rays of sunshine slanting through the open window. At the same time she became aware of a thunderous knocking on the door. 'Rise and shine, Liz!' came the all-too-familiar peremptory tones.

'Coming!' she called, and stumbled out of bed. Still half asleep, she pulled on bra and panties, white shirt and jodhpurs, slipped her feet into jodhpur boots. She was tying her hair back from her face with a ribbon as she ran along the hall.

Jarrah was waiting for her on the shady verandah. 'Morning!' He looked fresh and alert, hazel eyes alight with vitality. 'Did I wake you up just now?'

She threw him an expressive glance. 'What do *you* think? No one could possibly sleep through that uproar!'

He grinned. 'It worked, though. Let's get cracking, shall we?' As they went down the steps together he threw her an appreciative sideways glance. 'You dug up some riding gear for yourself?'

'Oh yes, it was all in a drawer in my room.' Liz had no qualms about making use of the garments that were necessary for the job of work she had taken on. 'I was just so lucky they happened to fit me.'

'They sure do.' She could scarcely believe her own ears at the warm note of sincerity in his accents. 'You look terrific!' His gaze was taking in Liz's face, still flushed from sleep, the apricot tan of her slender throat revealed by the deep V of her blouse.

Surprised and irrationally pleased at the unexpected compliment from *him* of all men, she couldn't help smiling back at him and all at once a strange and unbelievable happiness was surging through her, something that had to do with just being here with him. Everything around her seemed to take on a sparkle, the trees behind the homestead cut sharply against the tender blue of the sky, the early morning air incredibly clear. In this heightened state of awareness just strolling over the dew-wet grass towards the stables was a joy. To break the spell she murmured, 'Do you always start work at this time in the morning?'

Jarrah nodded. 'Yesterday I took one of the stock horses down to the beach for a dip in the tide to heal up a cut on his fetlock.' They had reached the weathered timbers of the stable buildings, and all at once his tones were charged with pride. 'Wait here and I'll bring your horse out to you.'

Flinging open the doors, he emerged a few moment later leading a big chestnut horse, the morning sunshine striking golden gleams in the silky tawny coat.

Liz caught her breath, staring in disbelief at the splendid animal. Mate! Her father's stock horse on the farm, the thoroughbred that he had hoped would one day be a famous racehorse, her own beloved companion of so many early morning rides! Her gaze went to the horse's leg and a scar left by a wound she had bathed and treated with medication for many weeks.

All yours! If he only knew! Liz was speechless.

'What's wrong?' His perceptive gaze went from the chestnut to her tremulous face. 'Don't tell me,' he hazarded shrewdly, 'that you two know each other— wait a minute! That name of his, Liz's Mate——'

'Of course it's him!' she burst out on a breath. 'I'd know him anywhere.' Excitement lighted her eyes and forgetting everything else she ran forward, standing on tiptoe to fondle the tawny neck. All at once her eyes were misty. 'It's Liz,' she crooned softly, 'remember? It tore me apart when I knew you'd been sold to someone else. I thought I'd never see you ever again, and now,' her voice lifted on a wave of happiness, 'here we are together again! It's going to be just like old times!'

She turned a radiant face towards Jarrah. 'You couldn't ever forget Mate, I know I couldn't! He's got such a great heart and he holds his head so proudly!' She pressed her cheek affectionately against the warm silky neck. 'My dad thought the world of him,' she ran on. 'He bred him himself and broke him in and he was sure his chestnut had a great future ahead in racing, once he got his chance. Only,' all at once her voice dropped, 'he never got that chance, not with us anyway! Dad was hurt in a tractor accident and after that he wasn't fit enough to keep on training Mate. I was away that year, I took time off from schoolteaching and spent a year in South-East Asia with the Volunteer Service Abroad, you know? When I knew Dad had sold Mate it broke me up, but it was too late for me to do anything about it.'

All at once her tones lightened. 'He knew me again, though—I know he did! To think that I'll be riding him again! I just can't believe it!'

'Brilliant.' Jarrah was looking almost as delighted as herself, she realised. 'This is great news! It's really going to swing things my way.' He was regarding her with immense satisfaction. 'Means I've got a head start when it comes to the beach races I've entered Mate in.' He grinned. '*Liz's* Mate! Things are working out even better than I'd expected.'

'You mean——' Liz's blue eyes darkened in puzzlement. 'Oh, I get it,' she said slowly. 'Now that I've got a personal stake in Mate's training you'll get better value for your money. Is that why you're looking so pleased with yourself?'

He eyed her quizzically. 'Something like that.'

Her high spirits dropped with a plop. Oh, she might have known he would be motivated only by self-interest. Somehow, though, a little of the sparkling lustre of the morning had slipped away.

Her lips tightened and she threw him a resentful look. 'Okay, boss.' She moved to pick up a plastic bucket. 'Is this Mate's first feed of the day? Shall I give it to him now?'

'That's the idea.' Jarrah stood relaxed, watching her.

When she had completed the task he brought out a fluffy sheepskin and a saddle and slipped a bridle over the chestnut's head. 'You know the gen?' He was taking a handwritten sheet of paper from the pocket of his cotton shirt.

'Do I ever? If there's one thing I know about, it's horse training!'

'Good for you, Liz! Now this is the timetable I've worked out for you. First thing every morning is trotting and cantering on the hard wet sand, then afterwards a walk in the water to cool down his legs and a walk home afterwards. Okay?'

She nodded, running her eyes over the paper setting out times and details of a programme of exercise, grooming and feeding of the horse during the entire day. 'Reckon you can handle it?' All at once she became aware that he was regarding her enquiringly and it came to her that in this one area of his life she happened to be all-important to him.

She schooled her voice to a nonchalant note. 'It looks to be just the usual training programme to me.'

'Not quite. Things are a bit different down here on the coast——'

'I come from a coastal area myself,' she shot back at

him, 'and don't forget he's my——' she broke off, then swiftly corrected her slip of the tongue, '*was* my horse and I know how to handle him!'

'That's good enough for me.' Did she imagine a sudden relaxation of tension in his expression? 'You've got yourself a full-time job, Liz, but after five o'clock your time's your own!'

'I'll be on my way, then.' She was getting ready to mount when he strode towards her. 'Wait—I'll give you a leg up. Or better still——' Before she could guess his intention he had swept her up in his arms and for a timeless moment he held her close, his hard muscular body pressed to her softness. 'How about this?' His deep exultant laugh sent a wild excitement singing through her veins.

In an effort to resist the raw force of his masculine attraction that was still stirring her pulses at his touch, the hard man-feel of him, she said in a rush, 'What happens if I don't meet with your approval in this job?'

'You must be joking!' He was regarding her with such unconcealed satisfaction that her heart gave a great leap, then settled again. The next moment she jerked herself back to sanity. Don't fool yourself, girl! He's only looking at you that way because he's found himself a trainer for his stock horse-cum-racing champion. So don't get any mistaken ideas on that score!

As the next few days went by and Jarrah made no attempt to accompany her on her daily rides along the beach or even to make a visit to the stables where she groomed and fed the chestnut, it was clear to her that he intended to leave the entire training programme of the horse in her hands.

Wouldn't you think, her thoughts ran one morning as she brushed down Mate's gleaming coat, that Jarrah would come down to the stables just once, if only to make certain I'm working along the right lines! Is that the only reason you want to see him? a small voice jeered in her mind. Of course, what else?

At the dinner table at night there seemed always to be various men present, a farm advisory officer, a stock agent, a vet with whom Jarrah was engaged in conversation. Afterwards the men would vanish into the billiards room of the old station homestead. Not that I want to be with him all that much, she told herself, it's just that I'd like to know if he's satisfied with results. *Or with you*? She thrust away the ridiculous thought and went on feeding Mate.

Late one afternoon she was picking up a heavy rug in readiness for putting the horse away for the night when Jarrah came striding across the grass and into the yard where she was working. 'Here, let me do that!' He took the rug from her, then dropped it to the ground and stood motionless, his attention riveted on the shining silkiness of the chestnut coat she had spent the last thirty minutes in grooming. Then his gaze moved down to take in the horse's well-oiled hoofs.

All at once she caught the flash of white teeth in his sun-bronzed face and there was no mistaking the glowing appreciation in his eyes. 'Looks a picture, doesn't he?'

Liz nodded, trying to hide the tide of pleasure that was engulfing her senses. So he had noticed the results of her daily grooming, the hosing, the combing and brushing of the creamy mane and tail. The next moment, as she met the warmth of his glance, a thrill of excitement tingled through her. His deep tones, vibrant with emotion, reached her. 'Right from the start I knew you were the one for me!'

For a crazy second her mind took in the words without registering their real meaning. Then she did a double take and all the sparkle died out of her eyes. She should be accustomed by now, she reminded herself, to his flattering statements about her that were really no more than his congratulating himself on how smart he had been in having found a suitable trainer for his thoroughbred.

'You'd better wait and see how I get on with Mate at the beach races,' she told him crisply, 'before you congratulate yourself! For all you know I might let you down badly!'

'*You*? *Let me down*?' At the deep glow in his eyes her spirits see-sawed once again. 'Not on your life! Win or lose, you'll get the best out of him. I'll tell you something, Liz—you two make a great team!'

I'd rather it were a man-and-woman team! Now where in the world could that crazy thought have come from? Turning her face aside, she said huskily, 'How do you know? You haven't seen Mate and me in action yet!'

Jarrah gave a shout of laughter. 'That's what you think! Every man on the station has seen you and Mate down on the beach, up in the paddocks, in the yard. Some of those jumps you took him over logs and gates and fences have been terrific!'

Liz tried to make a joke of it. 'So you've been keeping an eye on me. And I never knew you cared,' she mocked.

His eyes seemed to soften, darken. 'You happen to be important to me.'

'Of course!' The taunting words came to her lips unbidden. 'The made-to-measure jockey syndrome! How could I forget?'

His lips twisted sardonically. 'Not altogether.'

'What, then?' Her eyes were blazing as she flung around to face him. 'An acquisition!' The hot words were out before she could stop to think. 'That's all you think of me. Just as you'd feel pleased with a new farm tractor you'd got yourself. It's enough to damage any girl's ego. You still don't believe me when I've told you it wasn't true what Brooke wrote you about me. He——'

His expression was grim. 'I thought we'd got all that sorted out before.'

'Had we? But you still won't——'

'I got the idea you wanted this training work——'

'Oh, I do, I do!' Liz's voice was tense. 'It's just——'

'Right now,' he cut in, 'it's your job that's the important thing.'

'Don't I know it!' she said through clenched teeth.

Her thoughts were in a tumult. He made her feel so— so unimportant as a woman! She felt a hysterical urge to scream at him. 'Listen, just in case you haven't noticed, I'm a girl! But you never see me as anything but a jockey wearing silks and a peaked cap!' If only she could do something, say something, to change his opinion of her!

All at once a project that had long been lying at the back of her mind crystallised into a definite decision. She couldn't wait to prove to Jarrah that she was a girl who was planning to make a success of a career of her choice in a man's world.

She drew a deep breath. 'I'm glad you're pleased with the training I've been giving Mate. Actually,' she was finding it difficult to keep the note of triumph from her voice, 'I'm thinking of giving schoolteaching up and taking up something that I really like. Something in the horse riding line.'

All at once his voice sharpened. 'You're not leaving here in a hurry?'

'Not yet.' So that was what was on his mind. He was afraid of losing her services as his trainer. She might have guessed what his reaction to her news would be. 'It's just an idea I've had for a while. I'd like to run an agistment farm. You know? Resting and working hunting and thoroughbred and racehorses for trainers. That's why,' she was savouring to the full her moment of triumph, 'it's so good to know that you approve of my

training methods.' Straightening her shoulders, she
eyed him challengingly. 'Oh, I know very well that
because of my age I'll have to ignore all the sceptics
who'll tell me I might not know what I'm doing.' Jarrah
was looking at her attentively and she found herself
running on enthusiastically. 'I've always wanted an
agistment farm, but I'll have to talk my dad around to
the idea, and that won't be easy, especially as I want
him to let me use some of his land.'

Her young face was alive with interest, her voice
ringing with confidence in her project. 'I'm planning to
work or rest between one and six horses at a time. That
way I can really devote time to each one. I'm so lucky!
Our farm at home runs down to the beach and I can
swim the horses every day, especially the racehorses
that often get skin trouble from the hard summer tracks
and need swimming or exercise on the soft sand. I'll
have to get some land by the sea, it's a must for my
purposes!'

'You'll get it!'

Liz threw him a suspicious glance. Was he mocking
her for her grandiose plans? She couldn't tell by his
expression, and giving him the benefit of the doubt she
swept on. 'I can train the hunting horses on the hills.
You know the sort of thing I mean? Some horses could
stay for a month, some for just ten days or so. It would
be a sort of holiday for them.'

'Like you at Hauturu?' came the drawling tones. Now
she had no doubt of the glint of amusement in his eyes,
and her soft lips firmed in exasperation. She could have
thrown the horse brush at him! She had confided to him
her dream and he was mocking her! She tossed her
head. 'I'm just telling you about this,' her voice was hot
with resentment, 'for the future. You might be looking
for some place to send your horses to one day.'

'Thanks for the tip!' She didn't trust the ironic

expression in his hazel eyes one little bit. 'But I happen to have a better idea, a long-term plan when it comes to looking after any horses of mine that need a holiday, as you put it. No, no,' he protested, grinning as she opened her lips to query his statement, 'I can't let you in on that one. Not yet. It's top secret!'

He was making fun of her, of course, she thought angrily. Oh, she might have known he wouldn't take her confidence seriously. Suddenly a thought struck her and she faced him defiantly. 'If you're throwing off at my wanting to run an agistment farm, just because I happen to be a woman——' To her chagrin she found herself unable to meet his mocking gaze and she turned her face aside. She was unaware that to the man watching her the softly flushed cheeks and the slender line of her throat made her look very young and appealing—and vulnerable.

'I'll tell you something!' She flung around to face him. 'Being a woman doesn't affect my decision in any way at all! Anyway, I always think women have more affinity with horses than men!'

'I'm right with you there!'

She looked at him doubtfully, but his expression was unreadable. 'You haven't put Mate's rug on him yet,' she reminded him coldly.

'Coming up! Here you are, feller!' Jarrah was lifting the thick cover lying on the floor of the stable and throwing it over the chestnut's silky back. Soon he had closed the wide doors of the building and they strolled in silence back to the house.

Liz could feel her cheeks still burning with anger. She couldn't imagine, she chided herself, what could have got into her to have actually wanted Jarrah to come down to the stables and talk to her, tell her how delighted he was with her training programme.

Viciously she kicked at a loose stone on the pathway.

She had got her vote of appreciation from him all right, plus a whole lot more that she hadn't bargained for!

'You'll be coming along to the woolshed dance tonight?' Mrs Malloy glanced up enquiringly from the scone dough she was rolling out at the kitchen table.

Liz shook her head. 'Not me.'

'But you must!' The housekeeper looked astounded at the unexpected reply to her idle question. 'You'd enjoy it! You'd have the time of your life there, everyone does!'

Liz searched her mind for a convincing excuse for her lack of interest in what was plainly one of the social events of the year at Hauturu Station. 'I guess I'm just not in the mood for dancing. I think I'll give it a miss.'

'And dash the hopes of every young stockman and shepherd on the place?'

Liz swung around to meet Jarrah's lively sardonic gaze. He crossed the room to help himself to a can of chilled beer from the refrigerator. 'Believe me, it isn't every day of the week the guys have a new female face right here on the spot. Especially a girl who happens to be,' his cool glance roved over her resentful young face and slim body, 'young and lovely.' She hated him for the mocking note in his deep tones. 'Unattached too!'

To her chagrin she could feel the hot colour mounting in her cheeks. It was the implication of that stressed 'unattached' that was getting under her skin. What was the matter with her? she thought wildly. She never used to blush like this before coming here. But then, the answer came unbidden, no other man had ever made her so *mad* as this sardonic male who was so much in control of his isolated kingdom. He never missed an opportunity of getting at her, and all because of his utterly mistaken ideas concerning his precious step-brother's cancelled wedding.

With an angry bang, she flung down the cup she had

been rinsing at the sink and turned to face him challengingly. 'Too bad!'

'You surprise me, Liz.' He was regarding her with cool contempt. 'I got the idea you'd be glad of an opportunity for—fresh blood, shall we say? Wasn't that the big idea in cutting loose and drifting around the country on your own, to have a good time? And to hell with everyone and everything else!'

She stiffened and flung him an infuriated glance. 'I told you before,' she said very low, 'that my trip was——'

'Now don't take any notice of Jay.' Mrs Malloy had evidently mistaken the rose flush in Liz's cheeks for nervous embarrassment. 'He's always teasing.'

'Teasing?' Recklessly Liz slapped down a saucer on the sink bench. 'Is that what you call it?'

Mrs Malloy threw her a smile. 'What he's really on about is that he's hoping you'll change your mind and come along to the dance tonight. That's right, isn't it, Jay?' she said placatingly.

'The more the merrier!' he observed cryptically, and moved towards the door.

The housekeeper's puzzled glance swept Liz's storm-tossed face. 'I'm sure he really likes you,' she offered inadequately.

'He's got an odd way of showing it, then!' Why should it matter to the boss whether she was at the woolshed dance or not?

All at once a resolute gleam lighted Liz's eyes and she tossed aside her earlier decision in the matter. 'You know something, Molly? I might turn up at that woolshed hop after all just to give the boss a surprise!'

'That's the spirit!' applauded Molly. She slipped a tray of scones into the oven. 'Don't take any notice of what Jay tells you. He never gives away what he's really thinking. When you get to the woolshed he'll be making a beeline in your direction, asking you to partner him in a dance. You'll see! He'll have to be mighty quick to beat the opposition though! What I'd give,' she murmured on a sigh, 'to be young again and to know all that I know now.'

'It's no big deal being young.' Liz's voice was rueful. Mentally she added, 'Especially when Jarrah is around!'

The housekeeper's mind, however, was running on other matters. 'I've got that new mail-order frock I haven't worn yet, the one with the grey background and the mauve-coloured roses pattern. Of course I'll only be watching the young ones dancing, but still . . .'

That evening when Liz had showered and dressed for the evening ahead, she was brushing out her long hair before the mirror when Mrs Malloy thrust her curly golden mop around the edge of the door. 'May I come in, Liz?'

'Of course.' Liz turned to greet her visitor. 'My, you're looking real smart tonight!' Mrs Malloy was wearing her new floral silk frock that she had ordered from a city store. Her golden curls were brushed into a halo around her head and she wore a string of amethyst-coloured beads around her sun-weathered neck. Altogether she looked extremely pleased with herself.

'Thanks, love. And that creamy muslin dress looks exactly right on you! It does ever so much more for you than anything you could have found for yourself in the rumpus drawer in your room.'

'Oh, that——' Liz's tone was careless. She was drawing the long strands of dark hair back from her forehead, gathering them together and twisting them into a topknot. A few tendrils escaped to cluster around her face.

'I wouldn't use anything from the drawer anyway,' Liz was securing the gleaming coil of dark hair with a jewelled comb that had once belonged to her great-grandmother. 'I don't need to, not now that I have my own travel pack—even if it does have only one party frock and this is it!'

'I know you Liz!' The blue Irish eyes held a teasing twinkle. 'You wouldn't borrow anyone else's frocks, even if you had nothing else to wear. It's that fierce independence of yours,' Molly ran on in her shrewd outspoken way. 'It's got something to do with the boss, hasn't it? Although for the life of me I can't see why you should care——'

'*Me*? *Care about him*?' Liz swung around from the mirror. 'What on earth,' she demanded indignantly, 'could have given you that crazy idea?' She clasped around her neck a chain with a small gold cross that was her single piece of jewellery. 'I don't feel that way about him now, not since I got myself a job here!' Her eyes glimmered with a secret triumph. 'Would you believe? I know he'd hate to admit to it, but he really needs me here to train his horse, and you know how much Mate means to him! For that he's dependent on me—on *me*!' She bent to slip bare tanned feet into string-coloured sandals. 'Believe me, Molly, it's a great feeling!'

'At that rate,' said Molly with a smile, 'he can't afford not to dance with you tonight!'

Liz straightened, lifting her chin a shade higher than usual. It was a habit she seemed to have developed since her stormy meetings with the boss. She said with assumed nonchalance, 'That depends.'

Molly looked at her enquiringly. 'On Jay, you mean? But surely——'

'No,' Liz said with spirit, 'on me! Whether or not I decide to dance with him. I haven't made up my mind about that yet!'

'He's a marvellous dancer.' Once again, Liz thought exasperatedly, the housekeeper appeared to have missed the point of the conversation.

'That's not what I mean,' she said.

A short time later when the two women went out on to the verandah they found a masculine figure waiting in the shadows of the bushes crowding the steps below. 'How are you, Mrs Malloy?' For Liz the boyish face parted in a cheeky grin. 'Thought you might like an escort over to the shed! It's Wayne,' he told her in answer to her puzzled glance. 'You brought the tea over to the woolshed for us. I was the guy at the sorting table, remember?'

'Of course!' All at once his open tanned face and friendly manner were familiar to her.

'Gee, you look terrific tonight.' His gaze was fixed on Liz as though he couldn't tear his glance aside.

She sent him a smile. 'You look slightly different yourself, come to that! No wonder I didn't recognise you at first!'

Out in the shadowy dusk the dark blue translucence of the sky was pricked by the first faint stars and light streamed from the open doors of the high building. They strolled over the sun-dried grass, threading their way through the cluster of vehicles that were parked at all angles near the woolshed, and soon they were moving up the steps of the woolshed and joining the crowd surging around the entrance doors.

'I don't believe it!' marvelled Liz, her gaze sweeping around the interior of the high-roofed shed where already guests were seated on long planks held up by hay bales that lined the walls. 'Of course,' she told the other two, 'I expected the floor would have been swept and the heavy machinery pushed to one side to make way for an area for dancing, but this—why, it's a transformation!'

High above, naked electric light bulbs were sheathed in coloured crêpe paper, trailing green creepers were

twined over rafters; and nikau palms with their great
ferny leaves, broke the severity of bare walls.

Liz's fascinated gaze went to the makeshift stage of
hay bales where two young Maori men with guitars
were joined by an older man with a banjo. The next
moment she noticed a group of muscular, deeply tanned
men who were standing a short distance away. 'That
can't be the shearing gang!' she said incredulously.
'They look so—different.'

'Civilised, you mean!' Wayne grinned. 'You've got to
be meaning my haircuts,' he told her. 'I'm not exactly
professional, but I do my best to give the customers
what they want. And I'm getting better all the time!'

Liz laughed, her gaze following the small children
who were gliding up and down the slippery floor. On
another level, however, her thoughts were with Jarrah,
her gaze roving the moving throng in search of his lithe
dark-haired figure.

At that moment she became aware of Molly, who had
laid a hand on Liz's bare arm, introducing her to two
young women, wives of the shepherds, who lived in the
bungalows a short distance away from the homestead.

'We were so lucky!' Susan, a plump pretty girl with a
dimpled face, looked, Liz mused, as though the
excitement of a rare social gathering had already
exhilarated her. She smiled across at Liz. 'There's a nice
new stockman who arrived at Hauturu last week to
work. He's young, but he doesn't dance, doesn't even go
for socialising—but brother, does he make a heaven-
sent baby-sitter! So Meg and me,' she nodded towards a
tall, serious-eyed girl at her side, 'we bundled the
children into bed at my place and then we took off. All
we hope is that no one ever teaches that boy how to
dance! For sure it won't ever be Meg or me!' Her glance
searched the rapidly increasing crowd. 'Jarrah not here
yet? Oh well, he'll be along soon, I guess.'

At that moment the band took up their instruments and the foot-tapping rhythm of a popular hit tune rose above the buzz of talk and bursts of laughter.

'Let's give them a lead, shall we?' Wayne had clasped Liz's hand in his and was pulling her along towards the cleared area of the dance floor. Almost at once other couples joined them and soon the scene was a shimmering kaleidoscope of colour and movement.

Liz knew that tonight she would have no lack of partners. A new girl at the woolshed dance would be an opportunity not to be missed by shepherds and stockmen in this remote and predominantly male domain. As her limbs moved to the beat of the melody, the thought intruded in her mind that the boss showed no particular interest in that direction. So far as she was concerned, apart from her usefulness to him as a horse-trainer, he regarded her as something of a nuisance around the place—and made no secret of his opinion. Unbidden, a memory of his brief caress flashed across her mind. Well, she amended silently, most of the time. Why was she thinking of him anyway? she chided herself. Most certainly he wouldn't be wasting time on thoughts of her! Or dancing with her either! Come to that, she was in two minds whether or not she would dance with him should he ask her. He didn't deserve it!

The throbbing beat crashed to a close, then after a brief pause music pulsed through the shed once again and she became aware of two young men who were converging in her direction from opposite sides of the room. But before they could reach her side, a young boyish figure was beside her. 'Dance?' Looking up into his bashful face she recognised the young stockman who had lent her his horse to ride the day she had gone to the gully to find Jarrah.

'Hi, Gary!' she smiled, and moved away with him, aware of his triumphant glance directed towards his disappointed competitors who were now seeking other partners who were less in demand tonight. As they mingled with the scintillating colourful throng around them Liz said laughingly, 'Were you standing behind me all the time?'

He nodded. 'Sure was.' He added ingenuously, 'I couldn't afford to take any chances of missing out.'

She eyed him teasingly. 'It was a bet, wasn't it?'

'Well,' he sent her a shamefaced grin, 'sort of.'

When the hit tune came to an end, Liz, flushed and breathless, moved towards the makeshift seating, but very soon the infectious beat burst on the air and once again she found herself besieged by eager partners who came hurrying across the floor towards her. It was a pattern that was repeated time and time again as the evening wore on.

Once between dances she found Susan at her side. 'I don't get a chance of a change of partners,' she complained to Liz, but her eyes were dancing. 'Duncan stays right beside me for every single minute and the other fellows don't get a look in!'

'Can you blame me?' Her young husband, lanky and smiling, slipped a possessive arm around Susan's waist.

Liz wasn't listening. She had just caught a glimpse of Jarrah, standing amongst a group of men not far away, and her stupid heart skipped a beat. Leaning forward, she peered through the crowd that was obstructing her view, to see him relaxed and smiling, apparently absorbed in the masculine talk going on around him and apparently not at all interested in seeking a dance partner.

All at once she froze. Could that have been her own name she had heard mentioned? Something to do with the proposed beach races? She strained her ears to listen and in a sudden lull in the murmur of talk and laughter echoing around her, she recognised Jarrah's deep tones

'Take it from me, that girl's out on her own. When it comes to riding she's got what it takes and a lot more besides! I've seen her in action and man, she's worth watching!'

There followed an unintelligible murmur of male voices, then one louder then the rest, carried clearly towards her. 'Beats me how you managed to talk her into taking the job, a treasure like that.'

Jarrah's tones, cool, offhand, smugly self-satisfied. 'She came to me, actually. Turned up on the doorstep one day looking for some place to stay.' A chorus of male voices. 'That you could be so lucky!'

'*Oh*!' Liz hadn't ever known she could feel so angry! She had a childish impulse to kick and scream. How dared he! How dared he give other people the impression that she had come to him, cap in hand as it were, begging the big boss for food and lodging! Well, didn't you? taunted a small unwanted voice deep in her mind. In a way, she conceded, but he makes me sound so darned pathetic! Oooh! She ground her teeth in helpless rage. She was feeling so incensed she wasn't aware that the infectious rhythm was once again echoing around her and couples were taking the floor. Nothing mattered to her right now but Jarrah and his cool assumption that he had practically had her made to measure for his own convenience. If she weren't bound to keep her word in the matter of training Mate, if she had any way of escaping from here, she would leave Hauturu tomorrow. She would——

At that moment she became aware that Jarrah had moved away from the group of men he had been with and was now striding purposefully in her direction. Erect, relaxed, all-powerful, no doubt he was about to perform his duty as host by asking her to dance.

Her heart was behaving crazily, and he had almost reached her when a plump swarthy man with a flushed face and hot blue eyes appeared suddenly at her side. 'Wanta dance?' His voice was no more than a slurred mumble and he appeared somewhat the worse for drink, but what did she care? He was her escape route and that was all that mattered!

She turned away with him a split second before Jarrah could reach her, and out of a corner of her eye she caught a brief glimpse of his dark face. Suprise? Disappointment? His expression was unreadable. The next moment he had paused beside a pale, nondescript-looking girl who had been seated near Liz. As if he would care that someone else had beaten him to the post! He had his lightweight rider he was so badly in need of, and that was all he cared about! Nor did it matter to her that tomorrow the report would be all over the station that Liz had turned the boss down for a dance!

She was relieved when the dance came to an end and her partner mopped the beads of perspiration from his forehead. 'Might as well get some fresh air,' he was saying, and uncaring where she went so long as she could escape Jarrah's attention, Liz moved with her slightly unsteady companion down the steps and out into the star-encrusted night. On the dried grass outside couples were strolling in the moonglow, dark shadows beyond the radius of the electric light bulb burning on the porch.

They had gone only a short distance away when he paused, putting a hand to his pocket. 'Wanta drink?'

She shook her head. 'Not for me, thanks.'

'Suit yourself.' He helped himself to the bottle. 'Been here long?' His voice was slurred.

'Not very long.' Something in the way his eyes were raking her warned her it would be wiser for her to keep him talking. 'My car broke down miles away from here and I'm staying at Hauturu until I can get it repaired.'

They talked desultorily and to Liz it seemed a long time,
until all at once strains of melody flooded into the
stillness of the night. She turned away in relief. 'Let's go
in,' she said.

'What's the hurry?' He lurched towards her unsteadily. 'Much better out here—with you!' He threw a hot
detaining arm around her shoulders. Ridiculous of her
to feel apprehensive about him. He was the worse for
drink, of course, and was behaving stupidly, but for all
that, he was harmless.

Other couples were moving up the steps and into the
lighted shed, and as Liz glanced around her she realised
that she and her befuddled partner were now alone.

'I'm going in.' In a deft movement she had freed
herself from his clasp, but it was no use, for the next
minute he had stepped in front of her, barring her way.

'No, you don't!' All at once his belligerent tone
changed to a wheedling note. 'Pretty . . . you're a very
pretty girl. Anyone ever tell you?'

Ignoring his amorous mumblings, she endeavoured to
dodge beneath his arm, but despite his inebriated state
he had anticipated her move. 'That won't do you any
good! You're staying right here . . . with me.' Suddenly
she found herself caught roughly to his chest in a grip so
powerful that her struggles to break free were ineffectu-
al. For whatever the state of his befuddled senses there
was no doubt at all of his physical ability to keep her
here.

'Nice hair,' she caught his muttered tones, 'I like my
women to have long hair!' Before she could guess his
intention he had reached with his free arm to fumble
with her topknot, roughly pulling away the pins to send
the curtain of dark hair cascading around her shoulders.

'Let me go! You stupid fool!' Wildly Liz beat her
hands against his chest, but his iron grip didn't slacken.
All at once his tone was hoarse and threatening.

'What d'you think I brought you out here for, eh? Come on now, a kiss——'

His flushed face was so close to her averted cheek she could smell his whisky-laden breath. 'No! Let me *go*!' In desperation she flashed a glance towards the lighted hall to catch sight of a tall masculine figure taking the steps two at a time. Could it be some deep instinctive longing that sent her cry echoing through the night, 'Jarrah!'

'Shut up, can't you!' A hand was flung roughly over her mouth, but it was too late. The shadow man was racing across the grass towards them and a minute later a strong arm jerked her free from her assailant. Then the red-faced, heavily built man, who had seemed to her to be so strong, was thrown like a crumpled dummy to the ground with Jarrah's well-aimed blow to the chin.

With some difficulty the stranger got to his feet, swaying unsteadily and pressing a hand to his bruised jaw. He turned aggressively towards Jarrah, but something in the younger man's threatening stance made him cower back. His surly vindictive tones were directed towards Liz. 'I know who you are. As soon as I saw you with your hair down I knew I'd seen you before somewhere. On your father's farm, it was. Had to get yourself away for a while, huh?' he sneered. 'Made a fool of yourself when you ditched Brooke, threw him over at the last moment before the wedding! Made a fool of him too. A good boy, Brooke, top rider too. He didn't deserve a girl like you!' As Jarrah took a menacing step towards him he backed away. 'Don't think you can fool me!'

Liz stood frozen.

'Get going, before I help you along your way!' At Jarrah's low threatening voice, the man, still mumbling, turned and began weaving his way towards a truck hidden in the shadows.

Over his shoulder he paused to throw a parting shot

towards Jarrah. 'Take my advice, mate. You'd best watch out for that one—she's tricky!' He stumbled away in the darkness.

Liz stood very still, a sick feeling lodging itself in her midriff. 'I suppose,' she jerked out bitterly, 'you'll believe what that drunken idiot said about me?' With a despairing gesture she pushed back the dark strands of hair that were blowing across her forehead in the night breeze. 'It's what you've thought all along, isn't it?'

'That idiot, as you call him,' his voice was steel, 'was good enough for you to come out here with and stay on when everyone else had gone back to the shed.'

So that was it. Her impulsive gesture in turning him down in the dance hall in favour of a drunken stranger had made him all the more inclined to believe that she wasn't at all a nice type of girl.

A cloud of anger mushroomed up inside her at the injustice of it all. 'Just because I turned you down back there in the shed for him——' What did it matter what she said to him? It was too late to mend matters. 'Aren't you going to say it?' she taunted him 'Get going, Liz, get your gear packed by tomorrow morning! I'll send a man to town to pick up the battery for your car and you can be on your way. Go on,' she glared at him with bright, challenging eyes, 'say it, I don't care!'

'Haven't you forgotten something?' There was a steely edge to his voice. 'We've got a contract that you train Mate and ride him in the beach races, remember?'

With a sick feeling of misery Liz realised he was speaking to her in the impersonal manner of an employer. He was determined to hold her to their agreement, no matter what.

'I'll stay, then,' she cried recklessly, 'but only because of Mate! He means a lot to me and I want him to win at those races just as much as you do!'

'Great!' Jarrah's carefully controlled tones struck a

chill in her heart. 'That makes you the right one for the job. I told you I was a good picker when it came to riders!'

'And I told you you weren't so good when it came to girl-friends!' The moment the words had left her lips she would have given anything to recall them. She had no idea she could be so vindictive, so bitter and horrible.

'Let's stick to horses, shall we?' At the barely suppressed fury in his tone Liz knew that once again she had touched a raw nerve. Strangely she felt no triumph in the knowledge, only a deep sense of remorse. An odd feeling of something precious, briefly glimpsed and now lost to her for ever. Why did it have to be this way?

He was gazing at her in silence. Could it be moonlight flooding the paddocks around them with silver that painted shadowed planes and angles on his dark face, making him look stern and unrelenting? The next minute he bent to pick up something in the grass below. Her jewelled comb glinted in his hand as he held it out to her.

'Thanks.' She thrust it in her hair and turned abruptly away from him. 'I'm going back to the house.'

His terse tones halted her. 'Aren't you going to say goodnight?' In a stride he was beside her.

'No, I'm not!' She faced him defiantly, the soft night breeze lifting the dark hair swirling around her shoulders. The nerve of him! The pressure of his fingers was digging into her bare arm. 'Take your hand away, will you!' she flung at him. 'You're hurting me!'

His pressure lightened, but she suspected that the slightest struggle to escape his detaining grip would render her once more a prisoner. If only she weren't so stupidly vulnerable to his touch!

'I don't have to do as you say!' she protested wildly, 'except about Mate——' She was finding it difficult to think clearly, her thoughts scattered by the disturbing

caress of his touch. Crazy! Crazy! The attraction that
drew them together, something she felt Jarrah too was
aware of, was taking over, weakening her defences, her
determination to take no notice of his commands, to be
her own woman at all costs. Difficult, though, when the
enervating sweetness that had been her undoing on
those earlier occasions was once more having its way
with her.

She couldn't seem to find the words to argue with
him, but it made no difference really because without
warning he jerked her roughly towards him. Then his
mouth covered hers with a savage passion which she
knew was deliberate. A bruising, punishing kiss
without tenderness or mercy.

When he let her go her eyes were wet with tears. She
flung the back of her hand to her bruised lips. 'W-what
was that for?' she asked shakily

'Just a goodnight kiss.' His cold sardonic tones cut
across her ragged nerves and from the mists swirling
around her she groped in her mind for sanity. 'It—
didn't feel that way.'

'Why are you trembling, then?' She flinched at the
contempt in his voice. All at once his tones were low and
husky. 'Or do you tremble for all the men you let kiss
you?'

'Oh, let me alone, can't you!' She flung away from
him. 'Goodnight!'

This time he made no attempt to detain her as she
hurried away. Pray heaven her still tender foot didn't
cause her to stumble on the uneven ground, rutted with
the hoofs of cattle over the winter rains. She couldn't
afford to have him pick her up, not again, not when his
touch had the power to affect her so crazily, sending all
her resolutions to have nothing more to do with him
flying all over the place like dandelion puffs before the
wind.

. . . be tempted!

See inside for special
4 FREE BOOKS offer

Discover deliciously different romance with 4 Free Novels from

Harlequin Romance®

Sit back and enjoy four exciting romances—yours **FREE** from Harlequin Reader Service! But wait . . . there's *even more* to this great offer!

HARLEQUIN FOLDING UMBRELLA— ABSOLUTELY FREE! You'll love your Harlequin umbrella. Its bright color will cheer you up on even the gloomiest day. It's made of rugged nylon to last for years and is so compact (folds to 15″) you can carry it in your purse or briefcase. This folding umbrella is yours free with this offer!

PLUS A FREE MYSTERY GIFT—a surprise bonus that will delight you!

All this just for trying our Reader Service!

MONEY-SAVING HOME DELIVERY!

Once you receive your 4 FREE books and gifts, you'll be able to preview more great romance reading in the convenience of your own home at less than retail prices. Every month we'll deliver 8 brand-new Harlequin Romance novels right to your door months before they appear in stores. If you decide to keep them, they'll be yours for only $1.99 each! That's .26¢ less per book than what you pay in stores—with no additional charges for home delivery.

SPECIAL EXTRAS—FREE!

You'll also get our newsletter with each shipment, packed with news of your favorite authors and upcoming books— FREE! And as a valued reader, we'll be sending you additional free gifts from time to time—as a token of our appreciation.

BE TEMPTED! COMPLETE, DETACH AND MAIL YOUR POSTPAID ORDER CARD TODAY AND RECEIVE 4 FREE BOOKS, A FOLDING UMBRELLA AND MYSTERY GIFT—PLUS LOTS MORE!

A FREE
Folding Umbrella

and Mystery Gift *await you, too!*

Harlequin Romance®

Harlequin Reader Service®
901 Fuhrmann Blvd., P.O. Box 1394, Buffalo, NY 14240-9963

☐ **YES!** Please rush me my four Harlequin Romance novels with my FREE Folding Umbrella and Mystery Gift. As explained on the opposite page, I understand that I am under no obligation to purchase any books. The free books and gifts remain mine to keep.

118 CIR FAUF

NAME _____
(please print)

ADDRESS _____ APT. _____

CITY _____ STATE _____ ZIP CODE _____

Offer limited to one per household and not valid for present subscribers.
Prices subject to change.

HARLEQUIN READER SERVICE "NO-RISK" GUARANTEE

- There's no obligation to buy—and the free books and gifts remain yours to keep
- You pay the lowest price possible and receive books before they appear in stores.
- You may end your subscription anytime—just write and let us know.

As she lay awake in the darkness her over-active brain went over and over the events of the night. Black mark, Liz. Her unfortunate interlude with the inebriated stranger would be one more proof to Jarrah of her bad character, serve to underline all his preconceived opinions of her. A good jockey maybe, but as a girl she was someone not to be trusted, especially where males were concerned.

All at once the tears came, choking sobs that caught her unawares. But she wasn't beaten yet, she vowed, wiping away the wetness from her eyes with her hands. Before I leave here for ever, she promised herself, I'll make Jarrah see me as the girl I really am.

CHAPTER FIVE

IN the morning Liz was glad of the routine training work that got her up and about at daybreak. She had slept fitfully through the night—the burning memory of Jarrah's bruising kiss had seen to that. As she rode along the lonely beach, hurtful thoughts faded and she became one with the early morning world where the only sounds were the murmur of wind-tossed waves and the crying of gulls wheeling in the translucent blue overhead.

A long time later when she returned to the house, she found Molly in the kitchen. 'Morning, Liz,' the housekeeper greeted her cheerfully, 'you'll be ready for a bite to eat.'

'Thanks, but I'm not hungry. Just a cup of coffee——'

'You're feeling all right?' Molly's tones were threaded with concern.

'Of course I am.' Liz summoned what she hoped would pass for a carefree smile. 'Never better!'

'Thank goodness for that!' Molly plugged in the electric kettle. 'You disappeared from the dance so early last night everyone was wondering where you'd got to. Susan said——' She broke off, and Liz could imagine only too well the words that trembled on Molly's lips. By now word would be all over the station that the horse-trainer girl had turned the boss down at the woolshed dance last night. 'What happened?'

'Nothing much. Just a headache.' Liz evaded Molly's shrewd blue eyes. 'I get them once in a while, but I'm feeling just fine now.'

'Such a pity you didn't wait a bit longer at the dance—guess what?' Molly's tones were laced with excitement. 'You missed meeting Bridget!'

She placed two cups on the table and seated herself opposite Liz. 'She only arrived in the country yesterday and do you know, she hired a car and a driver to bring her all the way up here from Wellington airport. Said she didn't want to waste a single minute of her precious time at Hauturu. Jay was still at the dance in the woolshed, but she wouldn't let me run down and get him, said she'd catch up with some sleep and see him in the morning.'

'Liz's eyes widened in surprise. 'You mean the girl in the photo on the wall in Jarrah's office? *That* Bridget?'

'My dear,' Molly chided smilingly, 'let me tell you that so far as Jay is concerned, there's only one Bridget in the whole wide world!'

For no reason at all Liz felt a chill in her midriff. For something to say she murmured, 'You weren't expecting her, then?'

Molly laughed away the enquiry. 'You don't *expect* a famous model like Bridget to arrange overseas trips beforehand, not with her tight schedule of engagements and the life she leads. She's so much in demand for assignments, photographic sessions, modelling at fashion parades, whatever. She just fits in a break here with us when she can juggle her engagements, and that's not easy for a model who's so much in demand. Over the last few years she's worked in New York, Paris, Berlin—you name it. Sometimes she even goes on assignments to places like the Caribbean. Can you imagine?

'She pops in here out of the blue. That's why it's such a lovely surprise when she turns up at Hauturu. She stays for a few weeks whenever she can get back here.

And being a famous photographer's model hasn't made one scrap of difference to the way she feels about her old friends.

'She and Jay both grew up in this district,' Molly ran on. 'Her folks owned a big sheep station not far away from here and when she and Jay were young children they both went to the tiny schoolhouse on her folks' property. Bridget is an only child, and when she won a national beauty contest here her parents were so proud of her. Then she went on to try her luck with modelling work in England and later on, her parents sold up their property and went to live in London too. She knows that Jay is always delighted to see her, and being a famous model hasn't made a scrap of difference. Bridget's not one to forget her old friends.'

Friends? Or old-time lovers? Could it be a warmer relationship, Liz wondered, that drew Bridget halfway across the world to this homestead in the lonely bushclad hills? She tried to push away a pang. It couldn't be jealousy, it couldn't—and yet . . .

'Bridget says she thinks of Hauturu as home,' Molly was saying. 'She——'

'Someone talking about me? I thought I could feel my ears burning!' An extremely tall girl stood in the doorway, stretching her arms and yawning. Reed-thin with irregular features, she had an oddly arresting face. The forest-green pants suit she wore complemented the cloud of coppery-red hair falling around her shoulders. Not beautiful, the thoughts ran through Liz's mind, yet there was something about her, a certain indefinable quality that marked her as a girl who would never fail to be noticed.

'Morning *again*, Molly!' A throaty laugh, a sleepy smile revealing small white teeth. 'I'm still only half conscious. All this time away I'd forgotten what really fresh air can do for me. I just don't need any more sleep—any fruit juice around?' Bridget had a deep attractive voice.

'Help yourself.' Molly indicated a glass jug standing on the kauri dresser. 'Bridget, this is Liz——'

The stranger tossed Liz a careless glance, then picking up a tumbler from the dresser she began pouring fruit juice.

'Mango-orange,' came the husky tones. 'Bless you, Molly! You remembered!' She threw the older woman a dazzling smile.

Bridget dropped down to a chair, her pale green heavy-lidded eyes flickering towards Liz, her disparaging glance taking in Liz's dark hair, wind-ruffled and beaded with sea-spray, the sand-encrusted faded orange T-shirt and white pedal-pushers. 'I guess,' she murmured indifferently, 'that you work here.'

'I do, actually.' Liz flashed the other girl an irritated glance.

At something in Liz's spirited tone Bridget's heavy-lidded glance lingered on Liz's young face, cheeks rose-flushed from the onslaught of stinging salt winds. 'A good boss, Jay, is he?' Her voice was careless.

But now Liz had her feelings well in hand. 'I guess so.' Carefully she made her voice noncommittal. 'I haven't been here long. I'm training a thoroughbred for Jarrah. He wants to put Mate in the beach races he's organising here in a few weeks' time.'

'Really?' Bridget's lazy tones registered polite uninterest. Clearly she regarded Liz's occupation as of too menial a nature to merit further discussion. The light green eyes appraised Liz's petite figure. 'Jay usually employs a boy to train his thoroughbreds. I suppose this time he couldn't find a suitable lad for the job, and anyway——'

Liz was hotly conscious of the other girl's slightly contemptuous glance, a look that said quite plainly, 'Not that he'd notice the difference!'

As if aware of a certain tension in the atmosphere, Molly cut in quickly. 'Coffee, Bridget? Black, the way you like it? I've got your favourite mango-flavoured yoghurt too.' Swiftly she ran on, 'You've come at the right time of the year, right in the middle of summer. You can relax and soak up the sunshine.'

'Not this time.' Bridget's husky tones were regretful. 'Right now dazzling bright sunshine is a no-no for me.'

Molly asked bewilderedly, 'What's wrong with sunshine?'

'Everything so far as I'm concerned,' Bridget answered in her low husky tones. Why must the other girl have that fascinating provocative deep voice, Liz wondered illogically, as well as everything else? It wasn't fair!

'I'm into something new,' Bridget was saying. 'It's quite exciting really. I've agreed to star in a TV movie that's to be produced in London in a month's time. The only catch is there's a stipulation in my contract that I have to avoid direct rays of the sun, especially the ultra-violet rays of the New Zealand sunshine. Seems the colour cameras can't cope with too much tanning. Oh, I know that artists rave about the dazzling quality of the light out here, but it's not for me this summer.' She added complacently, 'I have to take care anyway with this delicate creamy skin of mine.' She appealed to Molly, 'Know what I mean?'

Liz was acutely aware of the dusting of freckles over the bridge of her short nose, the smooth apricot tan of her body broken only by the imprint of her bikini. How clearly Bridget's words pinpointed her existence in another world, a life style so far removed from ordinary day-to-day living that Liz could scarcely believe it was real.

Molly was eyeing Bridget. 'Have you any plans for your stay here?'

'Not really.' Bridget poised her spoon over the carton of yoghurt. 'Most of the folk I used to know have moved away from the district. But luckily for me,' a secret smile played around her lips, 'not Jay. Oh, he might be Jarrah to everyone else,' she seemed to be speaking to herself, 'but he'll always be Jay to me. It's just something between us two——'

'And Molly!' Liz couldn't resist the remark. After all, any girl who thought as much of herself as Bridget obviously did deserved to be taken down a peg or two.

Liz caught a flash in the pale green eyes, but the next moment the fringe of gold-tipped lashes swept down to veil Bridget's expression. 'But of course you wouldn't count, would you, Molly?'

The words were softly spoken, but Bridget's glance, bright with malice, was aimed in Liz's direction. 'It's different with Molly,' she said tightly, 'she just works here for Jay.'

To Liz's surprise the housekeeper appeared not at all put out by Bridget's disparaging words. 'Everyone for miles around will be wanting to meet you again,' she said warmly, 'that's for sure!'

'They'll have to be lucky!' Bridget gave her husky laugh. 'I've got to get there first. One of the few times I'd wished I'd learned to drive a car. I never feel that way except when I'm back here in this country where distances are so horrific and the roads cut through heavy bush country seem to go on for ever.'

'Oh, for heaven's sake!' Molly disclaimed smilingly. 'You'll never have need to worry about transport while you're staying with us. Jay won't be able to wait to take you around the place, wherever you want to go. You know how much he thinks of you. There's not a thing in the world he wouldn't do for you!'

Bridget's smile, Liz thought, had all the confidence of a professional model. Sunshine flooding through the window sparked the cloud of shining copper strands to living flame and highlighted Bridget's flawless complexion. 'Maybe he's changed his ideas about me.'

'Like hell he has!' Jarrah was striding into the room, his eyes riveted on the tall girl who was rising to greet him. Liz could scarcely recognise him as the tight-lipped, angry man who had escorted her back to the house last night. There was a jauntiness in his step, a glow in his tawny eyes that she had never seen there before. He looked as though he were on top of the world, and why not? There was good reason for his elation. Didn't he have his picture girl right here in the flesh? A famous model who had crossed the world just to be with him. He had never looked at Liz like that and she knew he never would. Now where in the world had that ridiculous thought come from? As if she wanted him to look at her—that way. To hold her close in his arms, kiss her tenderly, the way he was kissing Bridget right at this minute.

'Welcome home, Bridget!' Even after he released her from his arms his eyes still glowed with that deep *loving* look. Just a kiss and a 'welcome home' kiss at that, so why was she feeling so let-down and resentful? Liz asked herself. And what concern was it of hers anyway?

'You look terrific!' The warmth in his eyes said a lot more. 'Even better than you look in that last picture you sent me.'

'Oh, that . . .' Bridget shrugged thin shoulders. 'You wrote that you wanted a recent photo, so——'

'Sure I wanted it. It's up on the wall in my office over

my desk where I can see it most nights.' The warmth of
his tone lent the words a special significance. His eyes
seemed to linger on Bridget's slightly crooked face as
though he couldn't bear to tear his glance aside. 'I'm
right with that guy who wrote up an interview with you
that was reprinted in our local papers, the one featuring
world-famous stars in the modelling profession. He
knew what he was about.'

Bridget's tone was vague. 'I've given so many
interviews——'

'Oh, come on, you must remember this one. It was
headed "What it's like to be at the top" and it featured a
picture of you——' The long smile lines in his bronzed
cheeks deepened, 'Bridget Amberley, famous model.
The girl you can't ignore.'

'And you should know.' Liz said the words under her
breath.

Jarrah dropped down to straddle a chair, his gaze still
resting on Bridget's face. 'Molly looking after you all
right?' he asked.

Bridget's pale green eyes swept up provocatively.
'Everyone looks after me at Hauturu, and I love it.
What do you think brings me away out here to the
never-never every chance I get?'

'Well,' came the rich masculine drawl, 'if you really
want the answer to that one——'

'No, no,' Bridget cut in swiftly, raising an exquisitely
manicured hand in protest. 'My secret——'

'If you say so.' But his eyes still glowed with warmth
and happiness and pride. Lucky Bridget, Liz thought on
a sigh, to have the world at her feet—and Jarrah too.
There she went again, she must be out of her mind to
think such things. She couldn't stand the man! But of
coure, she rationalised away her crazy imaginings, any

girl, any ordinary girl that was, would feel envious of someone like Bridget.

Jarrah's vibrant tones broke across her thoughts. 'How long can you stay anyway?' Of course he was speaking to Bridget, no one else in the room existed for him.

'Depends.' Bridget was studying her manicured fingernails. 'Up to a month, just so long as I don't get recalled to England in a hurry and sent to some fashion show in Frankfurt or Tokyo. You know how it is with me.'

'Make it a month.' He bent on her his deep indulgent glance. 'I promise you, you won't regret it.'

'As if I ever would! I've been here before, remember?'

'I've got plenty of plans, all sorts of ideas.' Jarrah's tones rang with enthusiasm. 'Wherever you want to go——'

Bridget sent him her brilliant smile. 'Oh, I don't need to go far afield for enjoyment. Just to be here, with you——'

'Whatever you say—Look,' all at once his tone sobered, 'I'm sorry about this. It's a damned shame, your first day here and I have to take off and leave you. I'm giving Rob McIntyre a hand,—remember Rob?'

'Rob?' Evidently taken by surprise, Bridget opened her lips to speak, then closed them again. The next moment her throaty tones were as measured as ever, and Liz wondered if she had imagined the startled wary expression in the other girl's eyes. 'Of course I remember him!'

'He left the district years ago,' Jarrah was saying, 'when his brother took over the family property. He was always one for the land, Rob, and he's been working like mad in an office down south ever since, saving every cent to buy up some property for himself. This year he decided to dive in at the deep end, give accountancy up and buy land up here. It's a place that's as isolated as they come, way up in the hills, but it was all he could afford. He'll have to put in some heavy slog to clear the bush and right now I'm giving him a hand. He's got a lot on his mind.'

'W—what's been happening to him? Don't tell me,' Bridget's husky tones sharpened, 'that he's found himself a wife at last?'

'Rob? You've got to be joking!'

All at once a mask seemed to come down over Bridget's face. 'Silly question. He was always so shy of girls years ago.'

'He hasn't changed,' said Jarrah, 'not that you'd notice! He's just the sort of idealistic fellow who'd fall hard when he does fall. But if he has any girl-friends he makes sure no one knows about them. He always was one to play things close to his chest. Even about that girl he met over in England——'

'England?' Bridget's heavy-lidded eyes flew wide open.

Jarrah nodded. 'He's been down to it ever since he got back from that tour with the agricultural outfit he joined up with. He was pretty uptight about what happened over there. I gathered it had something to do with a girl who'd let him down, or so he thought. He never did have much to say for himself, and since he got back from the overseas trip he's been all wrapped up in himself. He's sure copping all his bad luck at once, what with the accident——'

'Accident! Rob?' Liz wondered if she had imagined the other girl's quick intake of breath. And surely Bridget's face had paled. Even her voice was different, sort of hoarse. 'He's not—badly hurt, is he?'

'Good grief, no! Just hopping mad at being put out of action right now. He had an argument with his tractor on a steep slope, the thing turned over and he got the worst of it! He was lucky he didn't cop anything worse out of the crash-up than a broken leg. The hospital sent him home yesterday and he's getting around the place on crutches. His language is pretty choice!'

'I can imagine.'

'He's got a gang of Fijian labourers clearing the bush at the back of the property and I'm off to give him a hand in the steer-tagging department,' Jarrah went on. 'He's a proud devil, swears he can manage fine by himself, but if I go over there and get stuck in he can't do much about it!'

Bridget's green eyes still held their startled expression. 'Are you telling me,' she said slowly, 'that he's away in this isolated place by himself?'

Jarrah shrugged broad shoulders beneath his cotton shirt. 'More or less. That's the way he wants it. He's a stubborn cuss, always was.'

Bridget said in a low voice, 'Don't I know it!'

'It didn't help any when his housekeeper took off a while ago to live with her daughter in Sydney. Rob put an ad in the local rag: "Housekeeper wanted, good wages, etc." Only one woman answered the ad, and of course once she knew that Rob was away at the back of beyond on a place you could only reach by Land Rover on a road cut through heavy bush, she turned the job down flat. Can't say that I blame her,' he added. 'Life in a tumbledown old cottage with no mod cons hasn't got much going for it from a housekeeper's point of view. Don't look like that,' he ran on, 'he won't starve. He's got a couple of farm workers with him, oldish blokes who know the ropes, and they'll rattle up some meals. There's no electric power on the place yet, it's a do-it-yourself outfit, but Rob isn't too bad when it comes to looking after himself.'

'He should have found himself a wife years ago, then he wouldn't have all these problems,' Molly put in.

'You've got something there.' Jarrah's tone was thoughtful. 'From what I know of Rob, and I've known him for ever, he'd expect a lot more than that from the girl he wanted for his mate—a whole lot more!'

'Oh well,' Bridget appeared to have lost interest in Rob's love life. 'So long as he isn't badly hurt.' A smile played around her lips. 'Maybe what Rob needs isn't a wife but a good plain cook who doesn't care about being stuck in the depths of the bush.'

'Care to take on the job?' There was a teasing light in Jarrah's eyes.

'Which one do you mean?' Bridget flashed back.

'Which would you prefer?'

Bridget laughed, a deep throaty chuckle that Liz thought any man would find attractive. 'Me, I'd settle for the housekeeper.'

Jarrah's brows rose mockingly and Molly burst out incredulously, 'You? The famous Bridget Amberley working on a backblocks station? Don't make me laugh!'

'Oh, I don't know,' Bridget's husky tones took up the challenge, 'I reckon I could cope,' she appealed to Jarrah. 'Remember that time when I was only thirteen and Mum had a fall at the Hunt that put her in bed for two weeks and I took over the cooking and housework and all, and I didn't have any complaints——'

Jarrah laughed, his gaze indulgent. 'Guess the family didn't dare!'

'You'd be surprised,' Bridget ran on. 'That year the shearing gang arived bang in the middle of it all and I fed them too. And you know the vast quantities of food

those boys can get through in a day!' She added with
immense satisfaction, 'I coped fine, I really did. And I
could do it again—if I really wanted to.'

Of course, Liz thought uncharitably, you would!

'Good for you!' Jarrah seemed to find Bridget's
slightly crooked features more than fascinating. He
couldn't seem to tear his gaze aside. 'If you're finished
that bite of food you call breakfast——'

She sent him a rueful glance. 'It's a matter of
watching every mouthful I eat—I've got to in my line of
work. Sometimes I wonder what it's all for. I mean, you
only get your picture in a magazine.'

Jarrah's glance swept Bridget's sparrow-thin figure.
'If that's what you want,' he grinned, 'you make a great
job of it!'

'Thanks! But that's not what I meant. Know
something?' She smiled across at him. 'Sometimes it's a
temptation just to relax, settle down with someone I'm
fond of, away from the hustle and bustle of big cities.
Get out of the rat race. Eat what I like, do what I like,
live somewhere like this——'

'Now you're talking!' Jarrah's tone, Liz thought, was
warmer than ever. 'Let me know when you decide to
make the big break!'

'Oh, I will! I will!' Bridget's smile, Liz had to admit,
had something any man would find difficulty in
resisting. 'I bet you say that to all the top models!'

'Only the ones I like—— Look,' all at once his tone
was eager, 'why don't you jump in the Land Rover and
let me take you over to Rob's place, just for the ride?
You can help to cheer up the invalid.' He grinned,
taking in Bridget's arresting face. 'Chances are he won't
know you for the freckle-faced kid he used to know in
high school. Believe me, you'll make his day!'

'Oh, I don't know,' Bridget's throaty voice held an

odd inflection. 'I guess he'll know—who I am. Actually, I've caught up with him since then.' All at once she was speaking faster, winding a strand of glinting coppery hair round and round her finger. Her laughter had a forced note. 'Isn't there a saying that if someone from this part of the world goes to London, sooner or later if they wait long enough in Picadilly Circus they'll meet up with someone they know from down under. It's true, it really is, I've proved it!'

Jarrah's thickly marked brows rose questioningly. 'Funny, Rob didn't put me in the picture about that.'

'Why should he?' Bridget's tones were lazy once again. 'I mean, it wasn't important. We didn't see much of each other.'

Jarrah's appreciative glance rested on the girl facing him. There was a glint in his eyes and his well-shaped lips twitched at the corners. 'You can't tell me that was Rob's fault!'

'We—ll,' Bridget's provocative glance lifted to meet his teasing grin, 'what do *you* think?'

So Rob was just another male whom Bridget had enslaved with her aura of glamour and sophistication. Liz felt annoyed with herself, but the waspish thoughts kept sneaking into her mind, she couldn't imagine why.

Jarrah got to his feet and Liz noticed he still had about him that elated un-Jarrah-like look. 'Let's shoot through, shall we?' he appealed to Bridget.

'Why not?' All at once Bridget's face was alight with excitement and some other emotion Liz couldn't put a name to. With a fluid motion she rose from her chair and linking her hand in the crook of Jarrah's arm, she threw a smile over her shoulder. 'Bye, Molly!'

Halfway to the door Jarrah paused to jerk his dark head in Liz's direction. His glance, cool and remote, swept her face. 'How did the workout go this morning?'

he asked. 'You were a heck of a time getting back from the beach. Is Mate okay?'

His impassive tone chilled her. So he hadn't forgotten last night's little episode, she thought hotly. Not that she cared!

She threw him a level glance. 'Everything's fine.'

'That's all I wanted to know.'

Presently the sound of a vehicle starting up fell on the clear morning air and Liz, gazing through the window, watched as Jarrah swung the Land Rover round and took the winding drive.

Molly followed her gaze. 'I've never seen Bridget looking so happy to be here! It must mean something. Maybe this time she won't go back to London—ever. Jay seems to think the world of her, and you only have to see them together to know how she feels about him. Who could blame her? He's a special breed somehow, tough and tanned and wonderful looking—and he'd do anything for anyone.'

'Think so?' For no reason at all an icy wind seemed to blow over Liz's spirit. 'I wouldn't know,' she murmured repressively, and turned away from the window.

On the following morning when she returned from her workout along the beach she was surprised to find Bridget already in the dining room. The other girl wore a deceptively simple jump-suit of sand-coloured suede, her startling coppery-red hair swirled in a gleaming coil on the top of her head.

'Morning.' Bridget, who had been chatting with Molly, glanced up as Liz entered the room. 'You're the stablehand girl.'

As if she didn't know! Liz drew a deep breath. 'I'm training Jarrah's thoroughbred——' she began.

But Bridget wasn't listening. 'Like my suit? I designed it myself. I design all my own clothes,' she went on in the self-satisfied tones that were fast becoming familiar to Liz. 'Would you believe, I've never had a lesson in my life in dress-designing. With me it's just a flair!'

Before Liz could make any comment the slow tones went on. 'So if ever I decide to make my living in some other way, out of the public eye——'

'You? Out of the public eye?' Molly cried incredulously.

'Oh, you never can tell.' Bridget's tone was thoughtful. 'One of these days I might have to make the big decision. Right now, though, I have to keep my public image.' The green eyes moved to Liz. 'It's something you couldn't even imagine, my way of life. It's different with you . . . just a horse trainer——'

'And a damned good one!' Jarrah's deep tones cut in. He came striding into the room, aiming his sun-hat at the end of the dresser. 'Liz has got something! You should take in her performance on the training track one morning. She's out on her own, believe me!'

She was aware that his eyes were alert and full of light. Today he looked more than ever vibrantly alive, the male magnetism which she had been so aware of at other times so intense she could almost feel it. But it had nothing to do with her. His gaze was fixed on Bridget as though just looking at her gave him pleasure. 'How come you're up and about so early?' he asked her.

'Me?' Bridget's lazy glance lifted, her expression changing to one of sparkling challenge and something else Liz couldn't fathom. An unspoken message flashed between the other two. 'We had an appointment,' came the husky tones, 'remember?'

'Sure I do, but I didn't expect you to keep it, not so early in the day.'

Morning-fresh, Jarrah exuded vitality and a sense of

well-being. Why not, Liz told herself, when in place of
his cardboard picture he had the girl he loved right here
at Hauturu? And she wondered at the odd pang that
pierced her.

Bridget was smiling up into Jarrah's face. 'Oh, you'd
be surprised at what I can do if I really set my mind to it.
Especially,' she murmured significantly, 'when it's
something that's worth my while!'

All at once her low tones were threaded with
excitement. 'Jay's taking me for a drive around the
place,' she told Molly. 'Just catching up with what's
been happening since I was here last. Oh, I'd better
warn you, Molly, if we happen to run into people I
know, we might be away quite a while. Don't wait
dinner for us.'

'That's right.' Jarrah's tones rang with pride. 'When
you're escorting a famous model around her home
township it's hard to get away from folks. The old hands
want to catch up with the London news and new
arrivals can't wait to get to know her so they can spin a
line to their mates about having met the famous Bridget
Amberley. Can't blame them, can you?' The warmth of
his glance underlined his words. 'See you later!'

He hadn't even asked about Mate's performance
today, Liz thought stormily. Her lips set in a firm line.
Not that she cared! Close on the thought came another.
So that was the reason Bridget was so carefully dressed
and made up so early in the day. For looking up old
friends? Or for Jarrah's benefit? The truth was all too
evident!

The pattern of togetherness set by Jarrah and Bridget
continued as the days slipped by. They left the
homestead early in the day to return at nightfall or later.
Liz was inclined to agree with Molly's romantic
speculations. What else could she think? And why did it

hurt so much? For what had Jarrah's love life to do with
her anyway?

Often when Liz came in from her morning workout
with Mate she would catch a glimpse of Bridget seated
in the Land Rover as she waited for Jarrah to join her.
Invariably the other girl would acknowledge Liz's
morning greeting with a careless nod.

What right, Liz thought angrily, had Bridget to treat
her as some sort of stablehand in Jarrah's employ? Well,
you are, aren't you? argued a cool voice of logic in her
mind.

Not to him! As Mate's trainer I happen to rate pretty
big in his life. Her soft lips drooped. Even if he doesn't
approve of me personally!

Today she could hear Jarrah taking the verandah
steps two at a time. His sun-bronzed face alight with
vitality and happiness, his deep tones warm and eager.
'All set to go?' he asked.

'Ready when you are!' Bridget, wearing deceptively
simple casual gear, her porcelain-pale skin exquisitely
made up, smiled up at him from the Land Rover.

Jarrah went past Liz with a casual, 'Hi, Liz,' and a
quick inclination of his dark head. Clearly, she told
herself, since the incident at the woolshed dance, she
didn't register in any degree in his life, except in her line
of duty. Not like his companion, who even in the harsh
morning sunlight contrived to look almost unbearably
glamorous. No wonder Bridget had never learned to
drive a car when she could be out all day and half the
night with Jarrah, having fun. No gruelling training
hours for her! Moodily Liz kicked at a pebble lying on
the driveway. No hard-eyed accusing glances from the
boss either!

It seemed unbelievable to Liz that Jarrah, whom she
had imagined to be entirely taken up with the

management of his vast coastal estates, had now abandoned all his duties on the station in order to escort Bridget wherever she wished to go. Even the training of his thoroughbred in preparation for the forthcoming beach races had taken second place to the whims of his glamorous guest.

So Liz, working alone with her beloved chestnut horse, threw herself into her daily training programme and tried to ignore the strange feeling of desolation that had taken possession of her.

Oddly, Molly appeared to find nothing unusual in her employer's changed pattern of living. 'It's always the same when Bridget turns up out of the blue,' she told Liz. 'Jarrah drops everything on the station, even when Bridget comes at a busy season like lambing time or shearing, to spend the time taking her out, making sure she enjoys every moment of her stay here. While she's here he sees that she takes in all the shows in Wanganui.' So that was where they were when the Land Rover returned so late after a day's outing, Liz mused. Or was that the explanation? Liz brought her mind back to Molly's enthusiastic tone. 'Oh yes, Jay makes sure she catches up with everyone she used to know and doesn't miss a thing that's on at local theatres. There's so much she wants to see and do while she's here. And he's so proud of her! We all are!'

'Sort of local girl makes good?' There was a twist to Liz's soft lips.

'That's right.' Molly seemed not to notice the irony in Liz's tone.

The evenings that Jarrah and Bridget spent at the homestead followed the same pattern. No longer for Jarrah the masculine company in the billiards room of staff members or dinner guests. He preferred to stay in the softly lighted lounge room with Bridget, listening to

records, dancing to music from the stereo or just
chatting, apparently content to be in Bridget's company.

Once Liz came into the dusk-filled room to realise
that the other two were deep in personal talk, and she
didn't dare to reveal her presence in the room. The
curtains were not yet drawn and a rising full moon
flooded the sea outside with silver. Liz couldn't help but
overhear the feminine husky tones. 'Remember that
night in Monaco after your big race when we were
having a celebration? You'd won your event and were
given a monstrous silver cup, and I happened to be in
Monaco at a fashion show at the same time! Everything
worked out so beautifully——'

Hidden in the shadows, Liz caught Jarrah's deep,
heart-catching tones. 'How could I ever forget!'

Briget's throaty accents. 'And the night you caught up
with me in Paris——'

At that moment Jarrah rose to draw the curtains, and
Liz fled unobserved from the room. Friends? Or old-
time lovers? She no longer had any doubts on that score.
What she couldn't understand was why the knowledge
should hurt so much.

'Hi, Liz!' She was in the stables one morning, giving
Mate his early morning feed, when she caught Jarrah's
deep tones. She flung around to meet his smiling gaze
and her stupid heart gave a great leap. And she really
thought she had got the better of that madness! She had
to force herself to concentrate on his words.

'Still happy with the way Mate's going along these
days?'

'Oh, I am!' She was still bemused by his hazel eyes.

'No problems you want sorted out? Nothing's come
up that you can't handle?'

'Yes—no, that is——' Maybe this time he would listen to what she had to tell him, *really* listen! The eager words bubbled to her lips. 'There are so many things I wanted you to know about, not really important, but—— Today the tide was so high on the beach there was no wet sand, so I took Mate around the circuit. His time was just fantastic,' her blue eyes were alight with enthusiasm, 'the best ever! He——' She broke off, aware that his gaze had moved past her and that he was looking towards the house. Bridget was standing on the verandah, waving an impatient hand and clearly waiting for Jarrah's return to the Land Rover waiting in the driveway.

'Be with you in a moment!' His message carried clearly on the still air. Then he turned back to Liz, but she knew his interest was no longer with her, or Mate.

'What was it you wanted to tell me about?' he asked. 'Anything important?'

Her brief feeling of happiness changed to a sick sensation of disappointment out of all proportion to its cause.

'Okay then,' he turned aside, 'some other time.'

'No!' Suddenly Liz was angry. She hadn't known she could feel such anger! And as he moved away she decided to let him have it. 'Yes, it does matter!' she lashed out at him. 'It matters a lot!' Her blue eyes blazed with accusation. 'You asked me if I'm happy about Mate's progress, and I'm telling you right here and now that I am! I'm more than happy!'

Somehow she couldn't sustain his level gaze. It was easier to speak her mind, she found, if she turned her glance aside. She drew a ragged breath. 'The thing is, are you?' The injustice of it all got the better of her and before he could make an answer she burst out angrily, 'You haven't bothered to come and see Mate working for days and days, and he's getting on so well, even better than I'd hoped. His performance now is just terrific!' Swept along by her own enthusiasm, she ran on, 'At the rate he's going he's going to leave the other horses in his race for dead——' She broke off. 'Oh, what's the use of telling you all this? You don't care about Mate.' She added very low, 'Or me.'

'Why should I?' His deep chuckle, the amused lift of his well-shaped brows made her all the more enraged. 'When I've got someone on the job who's got it all in hand? Someone I can trust!' His vibrant tones softened, doing things to her, things against which she had no defence. 'Having you walk into the training job at the right moment was the luckiest break I've had in a long time! There's something about a girl's touch with a horse. But with you it's a lot more than that!'

It was too much! All that appreciation and praise and trust he was handing out to her, *as a thoroughbred trainer*. It made her *sick*. A sneaky voice popped up in her mind. And you know why? You want him to praise you for yourself, to love you, idolise you the way he does Bridget!

She took refuge in sarcasm. She never was very good at sarcasm. 'Thanks very much.'

Jarrah's searching glance took in the stormy expression in her eyes and the mutinous set of her soft lips. 'Now what's the matter?' he demanded harshly. 'I got the feeling you'd be happy for me to leave Mate's entire work programme in your hands. What more do you want?'

'You could come and see him work sometimes!' she flung at him. 'Take an interest. He *is* your horse. You——'

He was eyeing her narrowly. 'So that's it! Look, if that's what's bugging you you can have a half share in

Mate. How does that strike you?'

Liz tossed the words aside with a shrug of her shoulders. 'Thanks, but——' Two danger flags burned in her cheeks.

'Not good enough!' His voice was steel. 'All right then, how would you feel about a rise in pay?'

'No! That's not what I mean. How would you feel,' she burst out with feeling, 'if you put your whole heart, time and everything into training a horse you loved, and his owner——'

'*Part*-owner.'

She ignored that and rushed on, '—didn't even take the trouble to see how his horse was coming along!'

'Okay, okay,' he offered placatingly, 'I'll take a look at Mate one day soon, give him the once-over, check his times—that make you happy?'

'You don't have to do anything you don't want to,' she flung as him tersely, 'now that you're caught up with—other things—just to please me.' She added very low, 'I'm not a child, you know.' The moment the words had left her lips she could have bitten her tongue out. Suppose he formed a mistaken impression that she was actually jealous of the time he spent with Bridget? But she need not have worried, she told herself the next minute, he wasn't the slightest bit interested in anything she said to him.

'I don't think of you as a child, Liz.' There was an odd unfathomable note in his low tones and the way he was looking at her, his eyes veiled, thoughtful, almost—regretful. Like a man who was wishing that things could somehow have been different. Liz stiffened her feelings. Probably he was wishing that she were different, more like his beloved Bridget who flirted with him, dressed up for him and never ever argued with him. Bridget who at this moment was approaching the stables, although Jarrah seemed aware of her.

'It's okay, then?' His voice was so matter-of-fact that she wondered if she had imagined that strange unreadable expression in his eyes a few momens ago. 'That offer of mine to make you part-owner of Mate?' he was saying. 'Fifty-fifty share. Is that all right with you—partner?'

She said stiffly, 'I guess so. You didn't have to do that,' and turned away before he could notice the sudden trembling of her hands and the flood of tell-tale colour in her cheeks.

CHAPTER SIX

'Is anyone going along to the Maori concert tomorrow night?' Molly enquired over the dinner table one evening.

Bridget, who chanced to be back in time for dinner, looked up without interest. 'Not for me, thanks.' Her manicured fingers were busy peeling a rosy-cheeked peach plucked that morning from the orchard. 'I've been brought up around here, remember? See one, you see them all!'

'Oh, but this one is something special,' Molly demurred. 'The Maori folk who live around the coast have discovered they've got lots of talent and they've formed their own concert party. I hear it's really something, terrific singing and dancing and traditional costumes. It will be a complete change from anything in the entertainment world you could see overseas. If you don't go along you might find you've missed out on something really worth while!'

'I'll risk it.' Bridget shrugged thin shoulders beneath her filmy green caftan. 'No,' she ran on in her throaty tones, 'you can count Jay and me out on that one. Actually,' she sent Jarrah a meaningful glance from beneath thick brown lashes, 'we happen to have other plans for tomorrow night—right, boss?'

He smiled across the table at her, his glance softening. 'It's your holiday. Whatever you say suits me!'

Liz could scarcely believe her own ears. Jarrah, who was so autocratic where everyone else at Hauturu was concerned!

'That wraps it up, then,' he said.

Something about Bridget's calm assumption that Jarrah would immediately fall in with her slightest wish sparked Liz to say brightly, 'Well, anyway, I'm going along to the concert!' Becoming aware of surprised glances around the table, she added with assumed carelessness, 'I haven't been to a Maori concert for ever so long, not since I was on holiday in Rotorua ages ago.'

'No!' Jarrah shot out the word explosively, his gaze formidable, his lips set in a hard line. 'You can put that idea out of your head right away!'

'Not me!' She avoided his smouldering gaze. 'Once I make my mind up about anything, that's it. Besides,' deliberately she made her voice light and mocking, 'someone has to go along to represent the gang from Hauturu!'

Even without meeting his eyes she was acutely aware of his infuriated gaze fixed on her small square-jawed face. 'Too bad,' he mocked softly, 'that the bridge over the river is down. The timbers were weakened in that flash flood we copped last month, I got word about it over the grapevine today.'

'Oh yes, I heard about that.' Liz surprised herself at the nonchalant way in which the words came out. 'But that doesn't make any difference to me. I'm planning to ride along the beach.' She was enjoying her moment of triumph. 'Gary and Wayne were telling me about it today and we've decided to ride to the concert. From what they told me, the hall is four bays further up the coast and if we time things right we won't get cut off by the high tide along the route.' She managed a light laugh that sounded almost like the real thing. 'I'd hate to have to climb up those high cliffs and spend the rest of the night perched up on a ledge above the sea.' She flashed a challenging glance towards Jarrah's set angry face. 'I'm riding Mate,' she announced calmly, 'so I'll be safe as can be.' *As if you'd care what happened to me!*

Jarrah's jaw tightened ominously and she knew she had scored a victory over him. Serve him right, she thought vindictively, ordering me around in that high-handed way, telling me what I should and shouldn't do in my free time!

His angry silence said a lot more than words and her blue eyes darkened with puzzlement. Did he really intend to let the matter drop? Accepting defiance of his orders from a junior worker on his payroll was scarcely the reaction she had come to expect from the boss. She hadn't anticipated he would drop the argument so soon.

He didn't. For when the meal was over and the other two women had left the room she found him at her side. He seemed to tower over her menacingly and there was a determined glitter in his eyes. 'I want a word with you, Liz. You'd best have another think about that little excursion of yours tomorrow night.'

'Think so?' She made to turn away, but he grabbed her arm in a vice-like grip and steered her towards the lounge room with its uncovered windows and darkening scene of bushclad hills. Anger throbbed in his low tones. 'That's all off so far as you're concerned!'

'Why shouldn't I go?' Liz drew a ragged breath. 'And take your hand away from me, will you! You're hurting me!' Indeed his savage grip was biting into her flesh. At last he let her go free and she gathered her forces together. 'Because you tell me not to? Boss's orders?' she flared. 'Is that it?'

A swift upward glance made her realise that this time she had really got through to him. Swiftly she followed up her advantage. 'I don't see why——'

'Do I have to spell it out?' he rasped. 'It'll be dark as hell along that coast, all ten miles of it.'

'It won't, you know.' She made herself speak with the inflection of a long-suffering parent dealing with a tiresome child. 'If you're all that worried about it, I'll be leaving before sunset at a dead low tide and by the time the concert is over the moon will be rising. I know,' she added complacently, 'because I've checked it on my calendar.'

'And what,' he bit out, 'if the concert finishes earlier than you expect?'

'No problem,' she said airily. 'I'll just wait for the moon to rise.' The sense of triumphing over the boss was exhilarating and she was getting carried away by the novelty of the sensation. 'It's no use, you know. Whatever you say to me won't make a scrap of difference. I'm going to that concert, and that's that!'

'The devil you are!' Jarrah ground out the low words. Clearly, Liz thought, the boss didn't take defeat lightly. The thought went to her head and she heard herself saying calmly, 'Anyway, I don't know what you're on about.'

'You don't know?' he rasped. 'You little fool, Liz! Don't you see, you're risking everything!'

She forced the light note into her voice once again. 'What risk?'

'You haven't a clue about what that beach is like! You——'

'But I have!' she cut in. 'I often train Mate down on the sand.'

'Another eight miles on to the concert hall——'

'What of it?'

'You wouldn't know the hazards! You can strike just about anything along that coast. And you're talking about taking it on in the dark!'

'I keep telling you,' she flashed back, 'it won't be dark.'

'Dark enough. How about old wrecks half buried in the sand, trees fallen from the cliffs, rocks submerged for years and then uncovered by the winter storms, a big fish—and I mean big—stranded by a low tide and

washed up on the beach?' Anger flared in his eyes.
'Can't I talk any sense into you? I can't let you risk it!
It's a damned sight too dangerous.'

For a crazy moment Liz imagined him to be
concerned for her welfare. She must have been out of
her mind, she told herself, to think such things. Jarrah
concerned for her safety—that would be the day!

'I get it.' She swallowed the lump that had unaccount-
ably lodged itself in her throat. 'You're worried stiff
that Mate might get hurt, stumble on something hidden
in the sand. Well, you needn't concern yourself, he's
sure-footed as they come and he'd never let me down.
Anyway,' to her horror her voice broke emotionally, 'I
guess it's not me that you're worrying about.'

He said tersely, 'What do *you* think?'

She knew the answer to that one only too well.

She pulled her mind back to his deep tones. 'I'm
depending on you. I can't replace you, and with the
beach races coming up so soon—— Don't you see, Mate
and I, we can't get along without you!'

For a moment she was silent, filled with the happy
glow his words had brought her. Then the warmth his
compliment had given her died away, giving way to
angry resentment.

'I might have known,' she said thickly. Little
hammers of pain and anger were beating in her head.
'You don't trust me! I'd really appreciate it for a change
if you did.' The hot words seemed to fall from her lips
without her volition. 'It would be something new,
wouldn't it?'

Jarrah's voice was dangerously quiet. 'What do you
mean, I don't trust you?'

'You know you don't!' she flung at him. 'You never
give me a chance about this or anything else! You don't
even trust the boys!'

'That's right,' he snapped. 'I happen to know those

two. Not that the horses would object. It takes a mighty strong hand on the reins to hold them back on the homeward run. You wouldn't have the strength.'

'Try me! Anyway,' she rushed on defensively, 'I don't need physical strength to control Mate. He always knows what I want him to do, he just knows! He'd never bolt with me.'

'Nevertheless,' his tone was dry, 'I don't want you bailing out on the way.'

Liz said tightly, 'No, of course you wouldn't. Not with the beach races coming up so soon.'

'True,' he agreed.

His impassive tone sent sparks of anger shooting through her. 'You're wasting your time, you know, because I'm going along to the concert whatever you tell me. I don't know what all the panic's about. I won't be alone.'

'Unfortunately. You may have talked the boys around to your way of thinking, you'd be good at that.'

Liz flushed at the implication. 'What's that supposed to mean? If you're saying . . . if you've got some stupid idea that way that I——' She broke off awkwardly.

'Judging by past experiences.'

She flinched at the contempt in his voice. The reminder of how he really felt about her pierced her like a knife. Oh, he was hateful, hateful!

'They wanted to go!' she cried, furious with him for the assumption he had levelled at her.

His mouth twisted ironically. 'No doubt.'

All at once she threw discretion to the sea winds. 'You never believe me, do you?' she cried passionately. 'Just because of what happened before. One day,' she flared, 'I'll prove to you how wrong you are about me!'

'Great!' he mocked softly. 'I can hardly wait. Meantime,' his voice throbbed with anger, 'do me a favour, will you? Drop this crack-brained scheme of

yours before it's too late. You'll get yourself hurt, cop a
fall or worse, and that's the last thing I want.'

'What?' She eyed him in surprise. The sudden
excitement that lighted her eyes died away almost as
soon as it had come. 'Oh yes, of course, the races . . .'

'Right!' His intent glance told her tht he meant
business. 'Now that we've got that sorted out——'

'Have we?' She flashed him a challenging upward
glance and before he could argue further she ran on,
'I'm going.'

His eyes darkened with anger and the moment of
silence was somehow threatening. 'I'm telling you, no!'

'Sorry, boss,' she forced her voice to a careless note,
'but that's the way it is!'

'You're crazy!' The way he was looking at her she got
the feeling that it wouldn't take much to make him
resort to physical violence in an attempt to shake some
sense into her. Involuntarily she stepped back a pace,
avoiding his gaze. 'I don't know why you're making
such a thing about it,' she muttered.

'You haven't a clue about that terrain, that's why!'

She had an answer to that one. 'But Mate has! You
told me yourself that you'd been exercising him way up
the coast before I ever came here——'

Jarrah cut in in a tight voice, 'I happen to know every
inch of the beach.'

She scowled at him. 'And I know Mate! I feel safe
with him. I always will. I'm not concerned.'

His tone was steel. 'But I am!'

'You won't stop me!'

'No?' he taunted softly. 'And if I order you not to go?'

'But you won't, will you!' Her eyes sparkled defiantly
and she raised her small square chin. 'It wouldn't do you
any good anyway.'

'Don't tempt me,' he bit out gruffly.

Liz turned away from the angry flame in his eyes. She

was flushed and trembling, but she made her voice light and airy. 'See you in the morning!' and she left the room before she lost the advantage she had gained over him.

On the following day no more was said on the matter, and Liz decided that Jarrah had lost interest in her movements. As she tucked her cotton shirt into jodhpurs and slid her feet into boots in preparation for the long night ride ahead she congratulated herself that she had gained a victory over him. She had got her mount ready earlier in the day and the two young stockmen would be waiting for her at the stables.

The sun was setting in an orange haze as she left the house. Molly waved a farewell from the creeper-hung verandah. 'Mind how you go!' she called.

'Oh, I will! I will!' Liz went on down the curving driveway. The next minute she stumbled and all but fell into the arms of a man standing motionless in the shadows.

'Wow!' She caught her breath. 'You gave me such a fright!' But it wasn't fear but Jarrah's touch, his nearness, the electric excitement of being held close in his arms, that was sending her into a state of wild sweet confusion. It was only with an effort of will that she pulled herself free.

Striving for sanity, she said the first words that came into her mind. 'If you're trying to stop me from going to the concert——' She hurried along the driveway and he fell into step at her side.

'Why would I do that?'

Swiftly she glanced up at him, but his closed profile told her nothing. She didn't trust him in this mood one little bit. 'You didn't look all that taken with the idea when I told you I was riding along the bays tonight.'

'True.' His voice had a hypnotic quality, and here beside him she was finding it very difficult to maintain

her attitude of careless defiance. 'That's why I'm
coming along with you!'

'You are?' Liz couldn't believe her own ears. Jarrah
joining the party to the Maori concert tonight, after the
way he had lectured her about going! The next minute
the penny dropped. Three guesses, she told herself
scornfully, as to why he had decided to come.

She threw him an angry look. 'I suppose,' she flung at
him, 'you'll be right alongside me all the way along the
beach and back tonight, keeping an eye on me, making
sure I get Mate safely home again. You don't even trust
me as a rider!'

'That's right,' he said evenly. 'Not on a dark beach
you've never seen in your life before.' The sudden
softness of his tone all but undid her all over again. 'I
don't want you hurt.'

But it meant nothing, nothing. Liz wrenched herself
back to sanity. 'Of coure not! You've put me in the
picture as to just why you're so concerned. So you had to
come along too . . . too bad!' Anger and a sense of let-
down made her fling at him any accusation that came
into her mind. 'I suppose the last thing in the world you
wanted to do tonight was to come to a Maori concert—
with me!'

'Whatever gave you that idea?'

Oh, he was maddening! He was being deliberately
obtuse. You never knew where you were with him. But
she did know, of course she did! She meant nothing to
him. As a jockey maybe, but as a girl . . .

Something in her silence must have got through to
him. 'Now what's the matter?' he demanded 'You'll
enjoy the concert.'

'It's not the concert——' Liz began.

'And the ride will be no problem. I'll look after you.'

The nerve of him! 'Thanks very much!' But she knew
sarcasm was wasted on him. She hurried ahead to join

the two young stockmen who were waiting in the stables.

'Bang on time, Liz.' Gary led forward the big chestnut horse already saddled in readiness for the ride. 'Here he is, he's all yours!'

'Thanks a lot, Gary.' She placed her foot on the work-roughened hand he was extending towards her and leaped up into the saddle.

The youth jerked his head towards Jarrah, who was having some difficulty in getting his rearing black stallion out on to the grass. 'Funny, the boss never struck me as being all that interested in culture and all that stuff!' he remarked. 'He must have had second thoughts about taking off for the concert tonight.'

Liz fingered the reins. 'Seems that way.'

Wayne gave a guffaw. 'Guess he has to grab the only chance he's had all week to get a breather away from that clingy girl-friend of his. Man, does she ever give him the runaround! Out of the house bright and early and they don't hit the homestead again until dark! I always had the idea that famous models like Bridget slept in until all hours.'

'Not this one,' Gary chuckled. 'She's flat-stick trying to get her man! Can't afford to let him out of her sight for a minute!'

'Reckon he's not putting up much of a struggle.'

'Would you?'

'You've got to be joking! Myself, I don't go for that skinny type of female ...'

The boyish voices faded as Liz guided her mount out of the stables. Not far away Jarrah was running a soothing hand over the gleaming black shoulder of his stallion. 'Easy now, Mate, easy now ...' At the low reassuring tones the horse quietened and Jarrah turned to Liz. 'Right, we're away!'

She urged her horse forward, then threw a backward

glance to the two stockmen who stood watching them
go. 'See you down on the beach,' she called.

'Not this time!' To her surprise they waved her on.

Liz drew rein and glanced back at them in astonish-
ment. 'But aren't you coming to the concert tonight? I
thought——'

'Sorry, Liz.' It was Gary who answered her. 'Thought
we'd catch up on some shut-eye tonight instead.' He
sent her a prodigious wink. 'Enjoy yourself!'

'Have a good time!' Wayne chimed in.

'I'll try.' She waved them farewell with a gaiety she
was far from feeling. A good time! Trapped in the boss's
reluctant company for hours and hours and hours!
What a hope!

At that moment Jarrah's head-tossing mount once
again reared high in the air, but the man's strong hands
controlled the stallion and soon the horses were once
more pacing side by side as they took the pathway
curving over the grass and down to the beach below.

Liz said, puzzled, 'The boys were so keen about
coming to the concert tonight. I wonder——'

'They gave the idea away, changed their minds,'
Jarrah offered by way of explanation. Carelessly he
added, 'I put it to them that there was absolutely no
need for them to come along to keep an eye on you,' he
tossed her a sideways glance, the glint in his eyes oddly
unnerving, 'that I'd take care of that!'

'I'll bet!' She eyed him suspiciously. 'I still don't get it.
They were really looking forward to the idea, told me
they couldn't wait to see the concert.'

'Only,' his tone was uninterested, 'if you were going
along with them!'

'Oh!' Liz digested this information in silence. At last,
'Now I know what happened!' she flared. 'You *told*
them not to come with us tonight!' she accused.

'Why would I do a thing like that?' Jarrah's bland

tone was infuriating to her taut nerves. 'Their free time is their own to do as they like. It's over to them!'

'I know,' she acknowledged, 'but all the same——' She drew a ragged breath and strove for control of her temper, but somehow she wasn't making a very good job of it. 'I don't know what all the panic's about!' she flung at him, furious with him for his overbearing tactics. 'What does it matter who I ride with tonight?'

'It matters to me!'

'I'd have been fine with Wayne and Gary,' she insisted.

'I wouldn't bet on it!' There was a tense angry edge to his voice. 'Chances are they'd have jacked up their usual race on the home stretch with the horses bolting all the way along the beach and up to the stables!'

'Great! I'd have liked that! It would be fun! But of course,' her mocking tones were sharp with anger, 'that wouldn't have suited you one little bit! Mate might do himself a mischief, break a leg or something.'

'That's right.'

There was no doubt of his intention, she thought, tight-lipped. He was determined to escort her every inch of the way. Suddenly she was swept by an electric excitement. Just for that she would *make* him race with her before the night was out, see if she wouldn't. Boss or not, she vowed silently, he deserved to be taught a lesson!

CHAPTER SEVEN

DOWN on the darkening sands a strong wind sent breakers crashing up on the beach in a cloud of spray, and towering cliffs against the setting sun formed a landscape of forbidding beauty.

Liz, riding alongside Jarrah, was all at once piercingly *aware* of him—the strong profile that was outlined against the fading light, the rugged vitality of his lean frame, the easy way in which he sat his mount as though he and his horse were moulded as one. If only she could ride on with him for ever—— She brought up her random thoughts with a jerk. Now where could that absurd thought have come from?

To chase away the fantasies she turned a sparkling-eyed glance towards him. 'Race you to the rocks!'

'You're on!' In a flash they were away, urging their mounts to a fast canter and then to a gallop, spurts of wet sand flying up from the pounding hoofs as they raced along the short distance. At the great pile of black rocks at the end of the bay they drew rein.

'Neck and neck!' Jarrah cried exultantly.

'Photo finish!' Liz agreed, and they laughed together. Somehow tonight she was finding it easy to forget the way he *really* felt about her, the resentment she bore towards him. Well, most of the time!

They rounded the shaggy pile of rocks that were all but submerged in the turbulent surf breaking over them, then they were around the sheltering barrier, facing an open stetch of sea where the full impact of the salt-laden wind met them head-on, lashing their faces with stinging force. Liz's hair, torn from its confining pins,

streamed behind her shoulders in a black swirl and
ahead of them frail balls of spinifex bowled along the
sand.

'Looks like the place is really living up to its name
tonight!' Liz had to raise her voice above the crash and
thunder of the waves. 'Hauturu, the resting place of the
winds!'

His deep tones were tinged with surprise. 'How come
you know the Maori meaning of Hauturu? I didn't
know——'

All at once excitement, wild and sweet, was surging
through her. She turned a laughing face towards him.
'There are lots of things about me that you don't know.'

'Like what?'

'Well for one thing——' She stopped short. The
temptation to plead her own cause was all but
overpowering, but even in the fading light she glimpsed
the tightening of his lips and she knew that his eyes
would have gone cold and watchful with the look he
seemed to keep just for her. Instead she said lightly,
'Tell you some time!' She heard herself nattering on.
'I'm a schoolteacher, remember? I've learned Maori as
part of my job. I didn't mind, it's such a musical
language,' her eyes twinkled, 'and the Maori sayings
can really hit the spot. One or two of them could fit you
perfectly!'

Jarrah looked at her suspiciously. 'Such as?'

She laughed. 'Can't you guess? The Rangatira, the
Big Chief.' Her lips curved mischievously. 'And how
about, *ko te mana i a Kawara tou mana*? You are
powerful as Kawara with all his influence!'

'I don't trust you, Liz.' There was an odd unreadable
note in his voice.

'Don't blame me! I didn't invent the ancient Maori
sayings,' she pointed out. 'And you never did trust me

anyway, did you?' The words were out before she could
stop to think.

'Liz . . .' There was something in the way he said her
name, a sort of husky softness, that made her heart
plunge. But the next moment the wind whipped his
words away and she wondered if she had merely
imagined the unaccustomed cadence in his low tones.

Soon stars pricked the translucent blue-black of the
night sky as once again they followed a succession of
small sandy bays.

Liz was enjoying the ride so much she was almost
sorry when at last the gleam of a lighted Maori meeting
house near the shoreline pierced the darkness.

'So you see,' she told Jarrah triumphantly as they
guided their mounts over a sandhill and up to a grassy
expanse above, 'you had no need to worry yourself
about me, or Mate either, tonight. I would have been
quite all right with the boys. Don't you agree?'

He said tightly. 'I'll answer that one when we hit the
homestead again!'

Liz's soft lips firmed. It was no use, she could never
get the better of him.

They hitched their horses to a fence and she swung
around to find Jarrah waiting for her. He was looking
. . . just looking. She was unaware that the moon, a
shining disc rising above bushclad hills, silvered the
scene around them, throwing her vulnerable young face
into relief.

As for herself, the moonglow painted angles and
shadows over Jarrah's sun-hardened features, making
him look stern and withdrawn. Was he regretting his
choice of a partner tonight? she wondered. Wishing it
had been Bridget with her oddly arresting face and not
his cheeky young stablehand whom he was escorting
through the magic of the summer night?

Pushing away the thought, she went with him over a

track winding over dried grass that led to an enclosure
where trucks, utes and Land Rovers were clustered at all
angles close to the lighted meeting house.

As they went through the wide open doors of the
entrance Liz realised that this was a place where Maori
culture of long ago had been faithfully and lovingly
reproduced by Maori carvers and weavers of today.

Long carved timber panels decorating the entrance
depicted Maori myths and legends handed down by a
race who had no written language. Twisting sea-snakes
and lizards, and squat human figures with four-fingered
hands and gleaming paua-shell eyes, told of gods of
mountain and sea and forest, as did the panels of flax
woven in intricate geometrical designs.

Evidently they were just in time for the performance,
for even as Liz seated herself beside Jarrah on a long
timber form, lights dimmed and a Maori man with the
silvery diction of his race welcomed the audience. The
next moment a group of young Maori men sprang on to
the floor, woven flax skirts in red, white and black
shadings flying around their knees as they dropped
down to sing an action song. Moving their carved
paddles in perfect rhythm from side to side, they
simulated the long canoe voyages of their island
ancestors in their epic journeyings across the vast
Pacific in search of a new land. All the time their
melodious voices rose in perfect harmony.

Presently their place was taken by a fearsome-looking
band of warriors, young Maori men of splendid
physique with feathered headbands and bare feet, their
faces painted in immitation of the tatooed skins of their
forefathers. With horrifying grimaces and earth-shat-
tering yells they stamped their way through the
fearsome actions of a war dance.

Even as her eyes followed the wild movements and
threatening actions of the war dance, all the time Liz

was acutely aware of Jarrah, close at her side.

'Enjoying it?' he asked.

'Oh, I am! I am! I'm so glad we came here tonight!'

Immediately she realised her unfortunate choice of words. She looked up to meet Jarrah's ironical glance. And then it happened. A spark, a life force, unseen but potent, flashed between them and a tremor ran through her senses. With unseeing gaze she watched the group of Maori maidens who with native grace were dancing with undulating movements and swaying hips, their extended arms and quivering hands emulating the shimmer of heat waves on a summer's day. A delicious madness was taking over and Liz, thrillingly conscious of Jarrah's nearness, was scarcely taking in the actions of the Maori performers as they knelt on the floor to play a stick game as old as time.

And he wasn't even touching her! Just being with him was enough to send her into this state of elation, idiot that she was! It was no use, she told herself, she was in the grip of a delicious insanity, and she could do nothing about it. Nor did it help matters when a young Maori man with the glossy dark hair of his race and a voice that could touch the heart sang unaccompanied the words of a haunting love song.

> 'Turn to me
> I could die
> Because of love for you
> What is this within my chest
> That pinches so?
>   Is it love
> Or what is it
> When I look at you
> You turn away
>   But within you
> There is much longing.'

The poignant words of the melody stirred her in a way she couldn't understand.

When the concert was over they emerged from the meeting house to find the sky was packed with stars and the moon, riding high, threw a rippling silver pathway over the sea. The waves were a glimmer of foam washing up on dark sand.

The horses were still tied to the railings where they had been left, but there was no doubting their eagerness to get back to their own quarters. Soon the mounts were scrambling over a sandbank and leaping down to the beach below. It seemed to Liz that there was nothing but the empty sea, the moving line of white surf, no sound but the booming of breakers and the dull thudding of horses' hoofs splashing along the water's edge. The moonlight threw shadows of horses and riders on the dark sands as she and Jarrah rode on mile after mile, bay after bay.

'No need to give them the hurry-up!' Liz called over the roar of the surf.

For the stallion, eager to take off at speed, was giving a spirited display of temperament at not being able to gain his own way and Mate was pulling so hard on the reins that Liz knew she would have sore hands in the morning, but what matter?

The gusty wind was behind them as they rode on. It was incredible, Liz marvelled, that they had travelled such a distance. Where could the time have gone? The unbelievable clarity of the moon-washed night, the exhilaration of the long ride and being here alone with *him*, all went to her head and she gave herself up to the state of dreamy rapture.

Suddenly they rounded a point and a gleam of light glowed against the backdrop of dark bushclad hills. The homestead! Her spirits dropped with a plop. Where

Bridget waited. Bridget, whom Jarrah loved!

She shook her head to dispel the madness that had her in thrall. What had she been thinking of to allow herself to be carried away, to feel this crazy longing to be with Jarrah, of all men? Jarrah who had no time for her at all, as a woman that was, as he kept reminding her. The thought brought her to her senses like a dash of cold water thrown in her face. How could she have forgotten that she had promised herself that tonight she would teach him a lesson, show him that he didn't control her movements and it was time he realised it! To prove to herself and him that her stupid longing for him tonight was no more than a temporary weakness, she threw towards him, 'Race you back to the stables!'

She was off to a flying start.

'Come back, Liz!' His authoritative tones, borne on the wind, merely had the effect of spurring her on.

She loosened her grip on the reins and let Mate have his head. Indeed he needed no urging, the proud head thrust forward as moving with his long stride he splashed through the wavelets, sand and seawater flicking up from his hoofs as he thundered on.

'Liz! Come back!'

Fat chance! Jarrah's voice was louder now. Nearer? She leaned low over the saddle, clinging with her knees to the horse's wet flanks. If Mate wanted to bolt all the way home as he showed every sign of doing, she wouldn't hold him back. The thoughts flew through her mind. Even though the territory might be unfamiliar to her mount he was surefooted as they come, she would trust him anywhere, day or night. He wouldn't stumble over hidden rocks or fallen logs, not him!

Now the air echoed with the thud-thud of hoofbeats on wet sand. She threw a swift backward glance over her shoulder to see Jarrah approaching at a fast gallop behind her. But nothing could stop her now. She couldn't *wait* to beat the boss at his own game!

The brilliant moonlight threw grotesque shadows on the sand as they sped on. Suddenly a shadow darker than the rest loomed up before Liz, a fallen log lying directly in her path. There was no time to swerve, but she had faith in Mate. The next moment the big chestnut horse gathered himself to leap over the obstacle, landing safely on the other side. Then the race was on again. The sound of hoof-beats told her that Jarrah was narrowing the gap between them. Ahead, however, lay a long stretch of sand and now Mate was really extending himself. Liz's slender figure looked like a part of her mount as she crouched forward, dark hair flying in a cloud behind her. Her voice echoed over the sound of wind and waves as she urged the chestnut horse to a still faster pace. 'Come on, come on,' she encouraged. 'You can do it! *Come on!*'

All at once she and Jarrah were riding side by side, the sweat from the horse's flanks mingling with the foam from breaking surf. Mile after sandy mile, and still they rode on together. The homestead was close now and both horses were scrambling over a sandbank, then racing towards home. Now they had passed the homestead in a flurry of hoofs. Another minute or so, Liz told herself, and she would be at the stables—and victorious, please God!

As they neared the outbuildings, silvered in the moonglow, a wild excitement surged through her. Then Mate came to an abrupt halt at the open doorway and at the same moment, Jarrah's sweating mount reared to a stop.

'What the hell do you think you're playing at?' His voice crackled with anger. 'Didn't you hear me yelling at you to come back?'

She faced him, head held high. 'Oh yes, I heard.'

'Then why didn't you stop? You could have ruined everything!'

She said airily, 'But I didn't, did I?' Let him rant and rave, what did she care? She had made her point. She couldn't understand why she had no sense of victory, only a hollow feeling of revenge.

'You know how I feel about your taking those sort of risks right now——'

She tossed him a cheeky grin. 'What risks? I knew I'd be all right with Mate. He's pretty good at looking after himself.'

'Pity,' Jarrah ground out, 'that you aren't the same!'

'Oh, I was okay!' Some devil of retaliation made her add, 'So I didn't need you to come along tonight after all.'

'You were damned lucky!'

'Not really. I know my horse. Anyway,' two danger flags flew in her cheeks, 'I nearly beat you.'

'Nice try, Liz.' His lips twisted ironically. 'You sure can travel!'

All at once a monstrous suspicion crossed her mind. Her eyes blazed. 'If I thought,' her voice throbbed with emotion, 'that you'd *let* me——'

'Relax! It was nothing like that. I have to hand it to you, Liz, no one can handle Mate like you!'

Suddenly she was illogically, crazily happy. 'Like I told you, it's a two-way thing,' she said. 'We understand each other, Mate and I. We're sort of in unison, if you know what I mean.'

'I get it.' But she knew he wasn't really listening, and there was something in the low timbre of his voice, potent as a caress, that sent her rushing into speech.

'I'd better give Mate a rub-down.'

They led the horses into the lighted building, removing sheepskins and saddles. They were rubbing down their sweaty mounts when Liz, glancing up, met

Jarrah's glance and a quiver ran through her senses. His lean face was flushed from the long ride, his hair unruly, damp with sea-spray. For a magic moment he held her gaze and she saw his eyes darken.

'You'll do me,' he announced with immense satisfaction, and her traitorous heart gave a leap, then settled again.

The next moment she returned to cold reality, 'At the beach races, you mean?'

The look in his eyes could have meant anything—or nothing at all. 'What else?' he shrugged.

Damn him! She could have bitten her tongue out. Heart-catchingly attractive he might be, but there were times when she would like to wring his neck!

She finished rubbing down Mate and hung up the bridle on its hook with an angry clank. Jarrah made her more mad more often than any man she had ever known. So why, she wondered a few minutes later as they strolled back along the winding path, did she feel this wild elation? It was almost like—being in love! But that, of course, was absurd. She couldn't stand the man.

She tried to concentrate on his vibrant tones. 'I've got news for you!' he announced.

She thrust aside the illogical excitement that flared in her whenever she was alone with him. 'The beach races——?'

'How did you guess?'

'Easy.' How could she have forgotten even for a moment that the beach event was all he really cared about, apart from Bridget, that was? Why must she keep forgetting about the other girl? *You never think about me, not really*! A wave of longing swept through her. If only he had a word of praise for herself. She schooled her voice to a carefree note. 'You've settled on a date?' she asked.

'It's all organised. I got everything arranged just

before we took off tonight. I got hold of a few of the local guys on the buzzer and one week from today it is! Don't forget, young Liz,' his voice softened, deepened, 'that I'm depending on you to win. You and Mate together, we've got it made! You know that, don't you?'

'Do I?' A wave of longing surged through her. If only he had a word of praise for herself, not just as a rider. It was difficult to make her voice casual and non-caring, but she gave it a try. 'What makes you so sure?' she asked.

'Ask yourself! Top rider, top horse—and I happen to know you and your capabilities——'

The ache in her heart deepened. If only you did know me, the real me! Aloud she heard her own voice saying brightly, 'I don't think that's much of a reason! How about the rest of the field? There are other good riders around here, surely?'

'True, true, but not like you!'

All she could think of to say was, 'It seems to matter to you an awful lot, this race.'

'Sure does.'

Her light laugh sounded almost the real thing. Well, near enough. 'You're making me nervous! What if I come in second, or third, or nowhere at all? Last in the bunch? I guess I'll never dare to show my face at Hauturu ever again!'

Jarrah's tone was supremely confident. 'Impossible! Believe me, it's a piece of cake!'

'I'm glad you've got such faith in me!' Liz had intended the words to sound mocking, but there was a betraying wobble in her voice. To cover the tremor she said the first words that came into her head. 'And if I do win, what then?'

'Then——?'

Wildly she searched her mind for a suitable reply, but

all she could come up with was, 'The reward, of course. The special bonus.'

All at once his tone hardened. 'If it's money you're after——'

'No, no, I didn't mean that——' She broke off awkwardly. Confused by his chilling tone, she scarcely knew what she did mean.

'I get it.' He stopped on the path and instinctively she paused beside him. Suddenly the atmosphere was tense with emotion and she stared up at him. She knew instinctively that he was about to take her in his arms and she knew she didn't want him to kiss her with that savage intensity that she knew only too well.

'Is this what you want?' His voice was deep and soft, like a caress.

Almost without her volition Liz swayed towards him, then he was pulling her close. She gave a soft shuddering sigh and then his mouth was seeking hers, sending fire running through her pulses. All at once she was powerless against the intense delight of his closeness, the touch of his mouth, gentle on hers. Then the pressure deepened, sending tremors running through her. She could feel his heartbeat through his thin shirt and the blazing stars seemed to merge and dance in the sky. Swept by emotion over which she no longer had any control, her hand crept up to run her fingers through the thick dark hair at the back of his head.

When at last he released her she was breathing rapidly and there was a trembling in her limbs she couldn't control.

'Something in advance, just to go on with.' Jarrah's low tones seemed to her to come from a distance. He had himself well in hand, Liz thought with a sinking of her spirits, for his voice was no longer husky but faintly tinged with amusement. Or had she merely imagined that his tone had been husky with emotion? She was always imagining things when it came to Jarrah. Stupid her!

Shaken, she tried to control her voice. 'Bribery,' she said in a light careless tone, 'will get you nowhere!'

'No harm in trying!' His flat expressionless tone chilled her afresh.

As they went on towards the house Liz was silent, dazed with a shocking sense of disbelief. She had fallen in love with a man who had nothing but contempt for her, a man who was in love with another woman. She had to face the truth, no matter how hurtful, for to hope that Jarrah would ever come to care, *really* care, for his young jockey-cum-trainer was to enter wildest-dream territory.

On the steps of the verandah the air was heavy with mingled perfumes of pink jasmine draping the pillars and the scent of the white trumpet lilies that spilled their fragrance into the summer night. Liz was unaware of it, she was all too conscious of the overhanging light and her own hot cheeks that must surely betray her tumultuous feelings.

As they reached her own doorway she paused. 'Goodnight, Jarrah.' With an effort she forced her voice to a non-caring note. 'Next time I'll beat you on that ride back to the stables!'

'Sure you will,' she couldn't sustain his deep intent gaze, 'if I let you!'

Somehow she managed to force back the tears that pricked her eyes.

''Night.' He left her and went along the carpeted hall, whistling softly. The sound of the haunting Maori melody of love and longing touched her with a poignancy she could scarcely bear.

Opening the door of her room, she stared blindly into

the darkness. Anguish pierced her like a physical pain. What was a kiss to him? A nothing thing, something far removed from his love affair with Bridget. Something in advance, he'd said, with more to follow if she won his race for him!

Suddenly Bridget's tones, throbbing wih emotion, pierced her fog of misery. 'Oh, Jay, I thought you were never coming back! Something's come up—something terribly important! I've got to talk with you——'

Liz glanced back over her shoulder to see Bridget hurrying towards Jarrah. Her diaphanous négligé floated around her thin figure and the coppery hair flowed around her shoulders. The next minute the two went to Bridget's room and, stricken to the heart, Liz heard the door close.

Now at last she let grief have its way with her, throwing herself down on the bed, trying to muffle her sobs. She loved him, she really loved him, idiot that she was! Even though his life was bound up with Bridget, even though he had no real interest in her, still she couldn't help herself. Molly had been right about Jarrah, she admitted now. He was a special breed. But he was not for her!

Over and over again she argued with herself. Have some pride, girl! You don't have to stay. You're your own woman. You could leave Hauturu tomorrow. She would do just that! Determinedly she wiped the tears away with the back of her hand. Let Jarrah find someone else to win his precious horse race for him! But all the time, deep down where it counted, she knew she couldn't tear herself away, and it wasn't the beach race meeting that was keeping her here. She just couldn't bear to be away from Jarrah, from the sound of his vibrant voice, the lean strength of him, his hazel eyes that could glint with amusement or darken with anger.

Just a few more days, what were a few days out of a

lifetime? And so long as no one guessed her secret. Across the screen of her mind flickered a picture of Bridget's shrewd, sleepy gaze. Liz knew she would need to play her part well.

Somehow, though, she couldn't stop the tears that were trickling down her cheeks. At daybreak, a glance at her ravaged face reflected in the mirror filled her with dismay. She didn't as a rule use make-up except at night-time, but today she was glad of the covering cream that concealed the dark shadows around her eyes. The swollen, reddened lids she could do nothing about, but a touch of blusher hid the pallor of her face. There, that was the best she could do in the way of camouflage, and with a bit of luck she wouldn't run into Bridget this morning, or Jarrah. Jarrah. The thought of him sent an arrow straight to her heart.

Deliberately she stayed out on her early morning work-out longer than usual in the hope that Bridget and Jarrah would already have left the house together, as was their custom. But wouldn't you know, she told herself crossly, that they would choose this of all mornings to linger?

They met in the hall, and after one glance at Liz's ravaged face Bridget gave her low throaty chuckle. 'Good grief! Jay, take a look at Liz! The poor girl looks all in!' Liz was unhappily aware of Bridget's probing gaze. 'What were you thinking of, making her ride for all those miles to the concert?'

The thought flew through Liz's distraught mind that whatever problems the other girl might have had last night, they had been satisfactorily sorted out by Jarrah. For Bridget's tone was as supremely confident as ever, her condescending gaze resting on Liz's swollen eyelids making havoc of all her defences.

'I'm okay,' Liz muttered, and looked away.

'What's the trouble, Liz?' She was disconcertingly aware of Jarrah's intent gaze.

She knew she couldn't keep her face turned aside for ever, and suddenly she swung around to face him. 'There's not a thing the matter with me! Why should there be? I don't know what you're on about.'

'No?' His gaze was fixed on her face and she had a disquieting suspicion that the colour she had applied to her cheeks was now standing out against her pallor. 'I got the feeling,' Jarrah said in some surprise, 'that you were having one heck of a time! Thoroughly enjoying yourself on the ride.'

'Oh, I was! I was!' Liz took her cue from his words. 'The Maori concert was fantastic—out of this world— and the ride there and back was super!' She summoned the best she could manage in the way of a carefree smile. 'What do you know, Bridget? I nearly beat Jarrah back to the stables on the way home! That's right, isn't it, Jarrah?' she appealed to him.

He nodded. 'A photo finish! Couldn't have been closer! Not bad for a run along the beach in the dark.'

'Really?' Bridget raised tawny brows, her enquiring glance moving from Liz's face, flushed now, to Jarrah. 'Funny, I got the idea that was the whole point about you going along with Liz to the concert last night—to make sure there wouldn't be any mad race on the way back. What happened?'

'Nothing much. Just a fun thing!' His deep tones were offhand, as though, Liz thought, the matter were of no import to him, one way or the other. 'There were no prizes for the winner!'

Clearly, however, Bridget remained unconvinced. 'No wonder,' the slow tones were threaded with amusement, 'that Liz looks a complete wreck this morning!'

'Look!' Suddenly Liz heard her own voice rising high,

out of control. 'Do you have to talk about me as if I were a hundred miles away? Just because I happen to look a bit tired? And anyway, whatever I feel like it's nothing to do with anyone else!' She flung around and marched resolutely down the passage.

Bridget's husky laugh followed her, the feminine tones clearly audible. 'She's really uptight. Maybe the race home was too much for her! Or did you do something last night to upset her?'

Liz felt sick in her midriff. If the other girl only knew!

CHAPTER EIGHT

SLOWLY, slowly the days dragged by. Keep yourself busy, girl, Liz told herself. Don't give yourself time for the agonising thoughts to sneak through. All the time she was fighting a losing battle within herself, for nothing could assuage the ache of misery, the hopeless longing to be with Jarrah, to be loved by him.

Now she spent more time then ever away from the house, working out on the track with Mate, riding along the shoreline or down in the stables.

Jarrah had invited friends from other districts to stay at the homestead and attend the beach races, and Molly, involved in her household chores, was too busy to notice Liz's quietness of manner or the dark smudges around her eyes. Liz had little contact with the guests. Not that any of them would notice, or care.

The nights, Liz thought, were the hardest to bear. That was when the black cloud of desolation blotted out everything else in her mind. And then the tears came.

There were the dreams too, images of a future that could never have any substance The touch of Jarrah, the lean-muscled man-feel of him. She and Jarrah together, flesh to flesh, in the rapture of love's fulfilment.

In the morning cold reality would come back with a rush and with it the anguish, the longing for the unattainable. Was it always to be like this? And to think, she told herself wryly, that so short a time ago she had imagined herself to be in love with Brooke. Now she knew it was only her pride that had been devastated by his betrayal.

'Are you awake, Liz?' A thunderous knocking beat a

tattoo on her bedroom door. 'Today's the day,' Jarrah's deep tones echoed through the room, 'so no sleeping in!'

'I'm *not* sleeping in!' she threw back indignantly, irritated by his attitude that she wasn't to be trusted, even to getting herself out of bed on time. And today of all days!

Her last day at Hauturu. She would tell Jarrah after the race meeting was over that she would be leaving in the morning. After all, that had been their arrangement, so he wouldn't be surprised. If only it didn't hurt so much!

Think of other things, the day's programme—anything! It was no use, she couldn't prevent her thoughts from slipping back to Jarrah, and that way madness lay. Liz blinked away the stupid moisture from her eyes, grabbed a towel and made her way to the shower. Surely that would help to brace her for the decision that lay ahead. It didn't, for even as she slipped on bra and panties, pulled on a faded cotton T-shirt and frayed jeans, thoughts of Jarrah filled her mind.

With an effort she wrenched her thoughts aside and presently she was running down the verandah steps and out into the brilliant sunshine. A jewel-like day where each leaf on bush and tree glistened and the hills were sharply cut against the tender blue of the early morning sky.

Up in the hill paddock where she went to get her mount, she found that Wayne had already caught the chestnut and was leading him through the gate. Together Liz and Wayne made their way to the stables, and as Liz preceded the curly-headed stockman down the narrow winding path she forced a smile over her shoulder. 'Tell me, will your money be on Mate in his race today?'

'You bet!' A shy grin crossed his boyish face. 'The boss is sure putting his money and his faith in you and that big chestnut. Me, I wouldn't care to be in your shoes if you don't hit the winning post ahead of the rest of the field today!'

'Don't be a defeatist!' she threw back. 'Of course Mate will win. Boss's orders!'

'He'd better,' Wayne said wryly. 'Well, good luck!' He gave her a thumbs-up sign as he turned away.

In the stables Liz hadn't a great deal left to do in the way of preparation for her mount for the race meeting. Yesterday she had spent a long time grooming the horse, oiling his hooves and brushing out the flowing creamy mane and tail. Now all that remained for her to do was to remove Mate's cover, give him his first meal of the day, followed by a final brush-down.

She had all but completed her tasks when a shadow fell across the open doorway and glancing up she found herself looking full into Jarrah's eyes. For an electric moment their glances meshed and held, then Liz wrenched her gaze aside and made a pretence of being absorbed in her task. What was it about this man, she wondered wildly, that just coming on him unexpectedly could send her thoughts spinning crazily?

'Looks great, doesn't he?' His matter-of-fact tones broke across her confused senses.

'He always does.' She was striving to keep her voice carefree and even managed a light laugh. 'That's my Mate——' She broke off, then quickly corrected herself. 'That's to say, *your* Mate.'

'Come on now.' Jarrah was running a hand affectionately down the horse's silky chest and appeared not to have noticed her slip of the tongue. 'Don't give me that modesty stuff! The thing is,' his warm tones rang with pride, 'Mate has improved out of sight since you took him over. Looks, performance, the lot! And you know it!'

'Think so?' The warm glow his words of appreciation

had brought her gave way to a feeling of almost unbearable poignancy and she glanced away for fear he might catch the glint of tears in her eyes. Oh, he was expert at handing out compliments in her direction when it came to her working capabilities, but seeing her as a person, as a *girl*——

Even without glancing up she was intensely aware of his warmly appreciative gaze fixed on her vulnerable young face. 'You're going to win your race today, you and Mate. You know that, don't you?'

'Do I?' If only he'd give her one word of appreciation for herself. Pricked to anger, she threw him a challenging glance. 'What makes you so sure?'

'Ask yourself! I've got a top rider, an outstanding horse. I tell you, Liz, we've got it made! Don't think I haven't noticed the way you handle Mate, that light touch of yours on the reins. And the special sort of bond there is between the two of you.'

'Such praise!' She pulled a face at him, but beneath her mocking smile she was aware of a stab of heartache. If only his lavish praise was for herself, as a woman!

With an effort she pulled her mind back to the present. 'How about the rest of the field?' It was difficult to force her voice to a non-caring note, but she gave it a try. 'There must be other good riders in the race today.'

'True,' Jarrah still sounded supremely confident of her outstanding riding ability, darn him, 'but I happen to have inside information about that particular race.'

Liz raised puzzled blue eyes. 'What sort of—information?'

For a long moment he was silent and there was something in the way in which he was regarding her. A warmth and—something else, something that sent little tremors tingling through her. There was a half smile on his lips and the low timbre of his voice was like a caress.

'You really want me to tell you?'

'I——' The words seemed to stick in her throat. He was leaning against a post and her glance took in his lithe strength belied by his relaxed attitude. But there was nothing relaxed about the expression in his eyes. Tiny points of light flickered in the hazel depths and even though his voice had a lazy quality it was soft and warm—and intimate.

'I really do,' she said unevenly. The thoughts were darting through her mind and she had to moisten dry lips. Maybe now the miracle would happen and Jarrah would tell her he'd found out his mistake, that she was all that he desired in a woman, and more!

'That's easy.' His voice still held that low caressing note. 'I know *you*!'

Liz's heart was beating erratically as she waited. Now was the moment for him to explain how mistaken he had been in his snap judgment of her. Now that he had come to know her better everything would be different—different and wonderful. But as the moments ticked on he said no more and slowly, slowly she felt her excitement ebb away. Once again she had only been fooling herself into hoping, even believing, the impossible dream.

The sick sense of disappointment was overwhelming and she had to force herself to concentrate on the masculine tones. 'Simple, isn't it, but it's what makes the difference!'

'So *you* say!' Frustration and unhappiness made her lash out at him. 'I suppose you're counting on this win, seeing you seem to have talked all the staff at Hauturu into putting their hard-earned cash on Mate when he runs in the beach race today.'

For a fleeting moment she glimpsed an odd look that crossed his tanned features. Shock? Almost—hurt? But that was absurd. Nothing that she could say to him would touch his feelings. The next moment she told herself she must have imagined that sudden bleak expression. Not Jarrah, not just because of her! That she couldn't believe!

You could tell that he didn't care about her one bit, she told herself, for now he was looking as relaxed as ever, slanting her an amused glance. 'That's right,' he nodded in cool agreement. 'Not that any of them needed much persuasion. I put it to them that they can't lose if they keep their eye on you and Mate at today's meeting. Just to make quite sure, though, that you come in first——' Jarrah was reaching a sinewy arm towards a hook on the wall above him and lifting down a whip he extended it towards her. 'Better grab this and take it along with you. You just might need it when you get in a tight bunch near the winning post.'

Drawing herself up to her full five feet two Liz lifted her small square chin a fraction higher than usual and looked at him steadily. 'No, thanks!'

'Take it!' His voice held a formidable note.

'I told you, no!' She looked up at him, blue eyes blazing. He had a knack of sending her emotions flying out of control, something that had to do with the stern set of his jaw, the infuriating 'do-as-I-say' note in his oh, so quiet tones.

Her soft lips tightened. 'I won't use it!' The indignant words fell from her lips in a torrent. 'I've never used a whip on a horse and I never will! Like I told you, when I ride Mate we're in unison all the time! It makes me mad,' she cried, 'the way men jockeys whip their horses when they're racing! Not me! I know,' she threw at him, 'that you think I sit too quietly——'

'I didn't say that.'

She glared at him disbelievingly. 'You've been thinking it, though. All the men riders do!'

Jarrah said very quietly, 'I think you're a top girl and a top rider.'

'You don't really mean that,' Liz protested. Then, unable to stop herself, she ran on, 'Not the top girl part——' She broke off, aghast that anger and indignation had betrayed her into dragging a personal note into the argument. Worse still, she had given him the impression that she cared about his opinion of her— she cared a lot.

Wildly she hurried into speech with the first words that entered her mind. 'I don't think thrashing of a racehorse is necessary, not one bit, and if you don't believe me——' her eyes sparkled angrily and a rose-coloured flush deepened in her cheeks, 'I'll prove it to you!'

To her surprise Jarrah's lips parted in a grin. 'Good for you!' He tossed the whip into a corner of the stable.

She said very low, 'It doesn't matter to you, does it? Nothing matters to you so long as I do you proud today!'

He eyed her with maddening satisfaction. 'I thought,' he observed cheerfully, 'that you'd get the drift.'

'I should do,' she muttered crossly, 'you're always telling me.'

He ignored that remark, saying evenly, 'Molly's got breakfast on up at the house. Better make it a good one. Coming?'

The heavy silence lasted all the while they crossed the dew-wet grass and made their way into the house.

Presently Liz exchanged work-stained jeans for breeches. Then she slipped around her shoulders the silk jacket of gaudy pink with its scattering of black diamonds that she had spent so much time laundering and pressing. She pulled on riding boots and gathering up the long fall of dark hair, tied the strands back with a ribbon.

When she reached the dining room she found Bridget

seated by the window, her make-up flawless in the
sunshine that was streaming in, turning to flame the
glinting, copper-coloured tresses.

'Morning.'

Bridget made no answer and Liz's lips tightened. The
next minute she bit back the angry retort that had risen
to her lips, realising that the other girl simply hadn't
heard her. Bridget was gazing ahead of her, staring with
unseeing eyes out of the window, her scarlet-tipped
fingers drumming nervously on the arm of her chair.

At last she seemed to rouse herself from some inner
turmoil. Her eyes focused on Liz. 'Oh, it's you.' Liz had
never seen Bridget in this mood, the low voice lifeless,
her eyes dark with her own thoughts. 'For heaven's
sake——' Suddenly she darted an angry glance towards
Liz, her voice ringing with emotion out of all proportion
to its cause. Her wrathful gaze came to rest on Liz's silk
jacket. 'That shocking pink is the last shade on earth
you should wear. You've got far too much colour in your
cheeks for it. What on earth made you choose it?'

Liz glared back at her indignantly. 'It wasn't my
choice, and anyway,' she said with spirit, 'I don't see
how the colour of jockey silks can matter to a rider at a
race meeting.' She shrugged her shoulders beneath the
silk jacket. 'Pink, purple, blue, it doesn't mean a thing
to me. How could it?'

'It could mean quite a lot if only you were smart
enough to see it.' Liz had a feeling that the other girl's
unprovoked outburst was in reality sparked off by
something else against which she felt herself powerless.
'But I guess,' Bridget ran on contemptuously, 'that you
and Jay are two of a kind. All either of you care about is
a stupid little race meeting on a beach that no one
except folk in this district has ever heard of. Really it's
not of the slightest importance to anyone.'

'It is to me!' Unnoticed, Jarrah had come into the

room and for the first time when he was talking to Bridget, Liz caught a tinge of displeasure in his tone. The next moment, however, he spoke goodnaturedly enough. But of course he wouldn't find fault with anything that Bridget said or did, Liz told herself irritatedly. It was obvious to everyone at the station that where the boss was concerned Bridget could do no wrong. Well, not for long anyway.

She brought her mind back to Jarrah's vibrant tones. 'How about changing your mind?' he said to Bridget. 'Come along with us to the race meeting. You can give a hand when it comes to cheering the Hauturu horses along to the winning post!'

Bridget nibbled a thumbnail. At last she said restlessly, 'Why not? Anything's better than sitting around the empty house. At least there's a chance——'

Jarrah smiled encouragingly. 'You never know your luck!'

'Luck? What's that?' Bridget's low tones were bitter. 'I've given up even hoping.'

Luck! Liz felt the familiar stab of anguish. When Bridget already had Jarrah's love!

Suddenly Bridget threw up her head, the cloud of shimmering coppery-red moving around her shoulders. She seemed to have come to a decision, a glint of determination shining in the pale green eyes. 'I will come with you after all!' Her usual lazy accents were all at once tense and edgy. 'I'll let you into one thing, though, Jay, it's not the horses that will interest me today but who I'm with! When it comes to winning I've still got a trick or two up my sleeve,' her meaningful glance held Jarrah's gaze, 'know what I mean?'

'I can guess!' His eyes still had that soft, indulgent look. 'Why don't you give it a go!'

Forgotten by the other two, Liz pushed away the anguish that was threatening to take over. She must get

the better of personal feelings, just for today, just until
her race was over. For Jarrah's sake—— There she
went again. She must make herself forget him. She
wouldn't *let* the other girl's words spoil this last day for
her, she wouldn't!

With a sigh she buttered a slice of toast and gulped
down a cup of coffee. It was all the breakfast she could
eat this morning. Before Jarrah could lecture her on the
merit of a good satisfying meal before a long ride and a
beach race she excused herself from the table. 'I'll be on
my way.'

She hesitated, half expecting him to accompany her
to the stables, if only to see her on her way, but clearly
his attention was completely taken up with Bridget. 'I'll
get one of the boys to run you down to the beach in the
Land Rover,' he was saying. 'Molly can go with you—
that suit you, Molly?' he appealed to the housekeeper,
who was hurrying around the table gathering up plates
and mugs.

'Wouldn't miss it for anything!' Molly sent him a
beaming smile.

Liz turned away. What was the use of waiting for
Jarrah to come to the stables with her? Clearly he had
more important matters on his mind. He was bending
over Bridget, his dark head slanted to catch her low
tones that were obviously intended for his ears alone.

Liz picked up the peaked jockey cap from the
sideboard where she had tossed it down and pulled the
cap over her eyes, tucking away the strands of dark hair
that had strayed over her forehead. She was aware that
Jarrah didn't even look up as she left the room.

When she reached the stretch of dried grass beyond
the stables she found a scene of activity as young men
with sun-darkened faces, together with a sprinkling of
older men, wheeled and milled their steeds amongst the
throng of riders. Loud guffaws of laughter and personal

remarks regarding the ancestry of their steeds and riders echoed on the clear air.

Liz too came in for her share of derisive comments. 'You don't think you've got a winning chance with that chestnut nag, do you? You should leave it to the boys!'

She pulled a mocking face at the young stockmen. 'Jealousy will get you nowhere!'

'That's the spirit, Liz. Stick up for yourself!' Susan and Meg encouraged from their seat in a truck. 'See you on the beach,' they called to their husbands as the group of riders set off for their trek over the hills.

Liz had already saddled her mount and was tightening the girth when out of a corner of her eye she glimpsed Jarrah striding towards her. He came to stand beside her and her heart gave a crazy leap. Heaven only knew why, she chided herself, for his attention was on the chestnut's gleaming silky coat and combed mane.

'You've done him proud.' The look of appreciation in his eyes, the warmth of his tone went to her head and a dizzy happiness surged through her. She schooled her voice to a careless note. 'Just a job,' she shrugged.

'Rubbish! Not with you it isn't!' Wearing a light shirt and breeches, the top buttons of his shirt unbuttoned to reveal the strong column of his throat and the mat of dark hair on his chest, he looked to Liz at that moment almost unbearably attractive.

'Brought you these.' His commonplace words jerked her back to some sort of sanity. And only just in time, she told herself as she took from his hand the goggles he was holding towards her. 'They'll keep some of the sand out of your eyes.'

'Thanks.' Liz slipped the goggles into her pocket.

'Get this straight, it might help——' She was having difficulty in concentrating on the advice he was giving her. He was standing close, so close she caught the tangy fragrance of his after-shave lotion, but she was conscious only of his nearness. With an effort she concentrated on his deep tones. What was he saying?

'Beach races are a bit different from the race track. It's a hell of a temptation to cut corners, but cut it too fine or time it wrongly and a big wave will have Mate by the ankles.'

She nodded, only taking in half of what Jarrah was telling her. 'I get it.'

'Right! I'll give you a leg up!' He extended a strong well-shaped hand and she placed her riding boot on it, leaping lightly up into the saddle. Just a commonplace action, so why did the brief contact shake her composure?

Gathering up the reins in her hands, she smiled tremulously down at him. 'I won't let you down.' To herself she added, Not if I can help it! Somehow it seemed very important that she and Mate give a good account of themselves today.

He grinned up at her. 'What did I tell you?'

Presently they moved away together, Jarrah keeping a firm hand on the reins as his spirited stallion with his sideways gait kept pace with her own steady mount. Soon they joined the group of horsemen who were making their way along the narrow sheep tracks winding over the tumbled coastal hills.

CHAPTER NINE

OUT in the empty hills with the salt wind blowing across her face Liz felt excitement mounting in her. Just riding alongside Jarrah on this their last day together was sufficient to send her spirits soaring in bitter-sweet happiness.

She glanced across at him as he rode at her side. He looked happy and carefree, she thought, as though she had already won the race he set such store by. Or could his expression stem from his love affair with Bridget? Bridget who couldn't care less about beach races! Why should she when she already had the greatest prize of all within her grasp?

Liz tried to concentrate her attention on the dusty track as the party guided their mounts over sun-dried hills. The only sign of civilisation was an occasional glimpse of stockyards at the roadside, a homestead set high on a distant rise and a ribbon of metal road ahead with a signpost bearing a roughly drawn arrow and the words Beach Races.

The heat of the day was steadily increasing when at last the group of riders reached the crest of a high grassy hill. Jarrah reined in his sweating mount and Liz pulled in at his side, her gaze skimming the colourful panorama outspread beneath them.

'I don't believe it!' she exclaimed on a quick intake of breath. 'To think we've passed all those deserted bays, climbed all the lonely hills on the way and now wham! This! The crowds, the colour, the picnic atmosphere—way out here in the middle of nowhere!'

Her gaze took in the scene far below. Beyond the

163

breaking surf of the ebbing tide, a yacht with scarlet sails made a splash of colour as it moved towards the misty blue of the horizon. Along the stretch of white sand horsemen were moving and Land Rovers, trucks and cars were grouped on the hard wet surface.

'See the tent down on the beach?' Jarrah was saying. 'That's the equalisator.'

'Golly! You could have fooled me!'

'The dilapidated cottage up on the bank is in business today supplying fried fish straight from the sea, and the woolshed down the road is where the riders weigh in,' he added.

Soon the horses were plunging down the narrow winding track and as they reached the thick white sand below Liz glanced around her, taking in the heavy surf, the rippling blue sea pierced with myriad dancing diamonds of sunlight, the great crested rollers breaking far out from the shore.

On the beach a relaxed and informal atmosphere prevailed, and Liz found herself plunged into a scene of activity. As stockmen and workers on sheep stations scattered around the wide area of the isolated district rode their mounts towards the starting point, the air echoed with laughter and goodnatured shouting as the riders met in friendly rivalry for the races soon to start.

Trucks and horse floats and transporters were moving from the road on to the beach and men wearing wide felt hats were hurrying towards the large tent on the shoreline. Bathers in the clear sparkling water not far from the shore were coming in for the first race of the day. Small children were forcibly restrained from their activity of digging holes in the wet sand. A man with a loudhailer was announcing the start of the local Station Hack Handicap and men riding their farm hacks were assembling at the starting point.

The high hills above formed a natural amphitheatre

and on the grassy slopes red, yellow and blue sun-
umbrellas blossomed as families spread rugs on sun-
dried grass or grouped in the back of trucks as they
prepared to enjoy the picnic atmosphere.

The scene was bathed in hot sunshine, heat waves
shimmering in the still air.

Liz turned towards Jarrah. 'Where's the starting
point?'

'Just that piece of rubber attached to a fishing line.'

'A fishing line?' She was having difficulty in
concentrating on what he was saying. The warmth of
the brilliant sunshine, the holiday atmosphere, the
sparkling environment of this spot under the lonely hills
and Jarrah here with her, just for once depending on
her!

'When the start releases the rubber,' he was saying in
his vibrant tones, 'the field is away!'

Bemused by his nearness, once again Liz had to make
a conscious effort to listen to his words. 'Those two men
standing on the Land Rover, they place the winners
across two pegs, one of them placed out at sea. The
running rail is the sea—too bad for riders in the last
race. Judging by today's tide they may have to steer
their steeds through the wavelets—— Hey!' Suddenly
Jarrah wheeled his mount. 'That's my call!'

Liz watched him exchange his restive stallion for the
horse one of the shepherds from Hauturu was riding.
Hullabaloo was a sturdy bay stock horse that she had
seen Jarrah ride on the property. But that was before
Bridget's arrival on the station had given him a more
interesting occupation with which to fill his days. Her
glance followed him as he rode towards the woolshed at
the side of the road to be weighed in.

Liz tethered her mount to a fence and went with the
rest of the party from Hautaru to the large tent on the
beach and the long queue of betters who were

goodnaturedly awaiting their turn at the equalisator.

Rules were few and the atmosphere lighthearted.
Evidently the crowd had made the event a picnic
excursion. Starters included a mixture of stock ponies,
former racehorses and station hacks. The jockeys were
workers on sheep stations, most of whom had trekked
for miles through the coastal hills.

Liz had just received her ticket when the starter's
signal announced the start of the race and the riders
sprang forward. But Liz had eyes only for the lean dark-
haired man riding the big bay.

As the group of riders and horses bunched together,
and raced along the hard wet sand the thud of hoofs
echoed in the clear air. Then slowly Jarrah on
Hullabaloo was drawing ahead. Reflections of horses
and riders were mirrored in the gleaming sands as the
horses raced alongside the breaking surf. Liz held her
breath, for now Jarrah was forging ahead! 'Come on,
Hullabaloo! Come on!' Liz was jumping up and down
with excitement, clapping her hands, her voice raised in
unison with the roar of the crowd that mingled with the
dull booming of the surf.

Then the hoofs of the big bay station hack thundered
past the peg mounted in the waves. Judging by the
applause of the crowd waiting on the grassy banks, Liz
thought, there was no doubt that the stockhorse from
Hauturu had been a popular choice at the equalisator.

Jarrah's hand was raised in a salute to the crowd of
spectators. He sent them a grin, then turned and came
cantering along the wet sand towards her.

Liz's face was alight with the excitement of the last
few minutes. She raised shining blue eyes to his face.
'Congratulations! How did you do it?'

He smiled. 'Joint effort, actually.' The warmth and
softness of his tone made her heart do a crazy
somersault. 'If it hadn't been for you, young Liz——' He

broke off and she realised his attention had moved to the Land Rover that was plunging down a grassy bank and on to the beach below.

The next moment the vehicle lurched to a stop and Bridget stepped gracefully down and, moving with a model's fluid motion, came towards them.

'Sorry I'm late.' Ignoring Liz's presence, she came to stand at Jarrah's side, sun-fired hair blowing around her shoulders. No wonder, Liz thought bleakly, that Jarrah saw nothing of his riding companions, herself or anything else. A chill crept through her body and there was a sudden tightenss in her throat.

How could she have been such a fool as to have expected Jarrah to seek her out in his moment of victory when Bridget was waiting for him? Bridget with her sleepy smile and sexy alluring tones.

'Anyway,' spots of colour burned high on Bridget's usually pale cheeks and her voice still held the edgy inflection that Liz had been aware of earlier in the day, 'here's wishing you luck in your next race!'

'Thanks. That goes for you too!' He was leaning forward in the saddle, his steady gaze holding hers, and once again Liz sensed a hidden significance in the conventional words. The removal of some obstacle standing in the way of the couple's future happiness together, perhaps? A cold hand seemed to close around her heart.

'I'll keep my fingers crossed—for us!' An odd unreadable expression crossed Bridget's face, then she turned away and Jarrah rode towards the Land Rover.

Fathoms deep in a sick feeling of let-down as she was, the chop-chop echo of an approching helicopter skimming the hills scarcely registered with her, and she was only half aware of the 'copter as it landed on the beach nearby, the crowd that had gathered around it keeping a safe distance from the whirling propellers and

stinging sand. Absently she watched as the pilot of the
'copter leaped down to the beach. Soon he was helping
down from the machine a tall, heavily built man who
was leaning on crutches.

The next minute Bridget was hurrying towards him.
'Rob!' Even from this distance Liz could see that the
other girl's smile was dazzling. 'You came! You came
after all!' The big man climbed into the waiting Land
Rover and the vehicle moved towards the grassy slopes
where picnic parties were seated.

A memory stirred in Liz's mind. No doubt, she
mused, the man on crutches was Rob McIntyre, the
New Zealand sheep farmer whom Bridget had known
long ago and met again recently in London. The tape
rolled back to that first day of Bridget's arrival at
Hauturu. She had seemed more than interested in news
of Rob and his accident. She had more or less admitted
that Rob had been attracted to her. Maybe the feeling
he had for the other girl had been something more than
that. It would be easy for Bridget to excite the feelings of
any man she cared to respond to. Look how Jarrah
worships her—swiftly Liz turned the dangerous
thoughts aside. Don't think of him! Get a grip on
yourself, girl!

With an effort she brought her mind back to the
present. Bathers had run back into the sea and children
too had taken advantge of the space between races to
play in the surf or dig holes in the wet sand. A shaft of
alarm went through her. Suppose Mate should step in
one of the hidden holes during his race? But he would
never do that. He was surefooted, and anyway the
dangerous depressions would be filled in before the next
race.

At that moment the Hauturu Cup was announced.
Some time later the equalisator closed and Liz realised
that Jarrah was riding his black stallion in the race.

As the line of horses started off she watched him. He was crouched forward, looking a part of his mount. Before long Jarrah was on the outside of a line of horses racing neck and neck, the breaking surf splashing up around Sultan as the horses pounded on.

The watching crowds were cheering, stamping, clapping as they called out the name of their favourite. Liz watched tensely as the main group fell behind and the two leading horses raced together, their images mirrored in the wet sand.

'Sultan! Sultan!' Liz wasn't aware of her voice raised excitedly as she shouted encouragement to the black stallion and his rider. She only knew she wanted Jarrah to win. Now the two horses, both black as night, both with a lengthy stride, were approaching the finishing line. It was impossible to tell which horse was the winner. A few moments later, however, the judges made their decision. Jarrah was announced as having gained first place, and the wild cheering of the onlookers left no doubt that the black stallion had been first favourite at the equalisator.

Out of a corner of her eye Liz was aware of Jarrah riding over the sand towards her. But she had no intention of allowing herself to be caught out that way a second time! Deliberately she pulled on a rein and guided her mount towards a group of riders from Tauturu Station who were gathered at the other end of the makeshift course. For a spilt second as she turned she had a moment's triumph on seeing Jarrah's expression of excitement give way to a look of surprise that was followed by a look of puzzlement, almost—disappointment. But he didn't have any need of her congratulations, she thought bitterly, not when he had the station staff cheering for him. And Bridget waiting for him in the Land Rover. So why did she feel no sense of elation but only a sick feeling of dismay as though in some way she had let him down, which was ridiculous really.

But she could no longer avoid him when a short while later he approached the group of young riders from the station. 'Molly's opening up the lunch basket over on the bank,' he told them. 'If any of you people are interested?'

'You heard what the man said!' The shepherds and stockmen rode away in the direction of the Land Rover parked on the grassy slopes. 'Coming, Liz?' Jarrah tossed her a smile. 'Got to keep up your strength! Can't have you flaking out in the middle of your race. You're on the programme right after the lunch break.'

'I don't want any lunch.' Even as the words left her lips she realised how childish they sounded. 'I'm just—not hungry.'

'But you're coming with me. 'He laid a hand on her bridle and suddenly she couldn't meet the deep intent look in his eyes.

'Are you ordering me?' A silly trembling sensation was overtaking her, but she managed to sound cool and defiant, at least she hoped she did. 'My, my, victory has gone to your head!' She glared at him with stormy eyes. 'What does it matter whether I join the picnic party or not?'

He ground out, 'It matters! Are you coming?' His low tones were ominous. 'Or do I have to give the crowd a demonstration of how to carry off your girl when she's being obstinate?'

'I'm not your girl!'

'Are you coming?' He fixed her with his no-nonsense look and a muscle jerking at the corner of his cheek warned her she might be wiser to do as he suggested.

'Oh, all right, then, if you're making such a thing of it, I suppose it's important to you,' she burst out, 'to see that I'm in good form for the next race.'

Jarrah didn't answer, but the scorching look he sent her underlined her impression that she had made the right choice in going along with him. 'Anyway,' she ran on, determined to score some sort of victory in the verbal tussle, 'I wouldn't mind meeting Rob McIntyre. It is Rob, isn't it? The man that Bridget was friendly with when they were both in London?'

Now what had she said to displease him? she wondered, for his eyes had darkened formidably and there was a hard line to his jaw. 'What do you know about that?' he rasped.

'Oh, Bridget told me about Rob the day she arrived at Hauturu. She told us all about it, you and Molly and me. Why?' she asked innocently. 'Does it matter?'

He shrugged but made no comment, and they rode on together in an angry silence.

The picnic party, seated on rugs outspread on the grassy slope beneath giant sun-umbrellas, looked happy and carefree, Liz mused, as she approached the group. And the food that Molly had prepared for the race day picnic looked delicious, she thought a little later as she joined the group. There was crusty home-made bread, salads and sliced meats, golden-topped pizza pies and small rolls filled with asparagus spears from the garden. A woven flax bucket bulged with luscious purple grapes, apricots and early peaches plucked from the orchard. In the chilli bins were cans of beer for the men, fruit drinks and bottles of Molly's home-made ginger beer. Yet Liz had no appetite for the delectable array of food.

There was no doubt, however, that the rest of the party were enjoying the picnic. The atmosphere was relaxed and informal. Shepherds and stockmen from the station, having collected their winnings after Jarrah's two races, were in high spirits.

The shepherds' wives, Susan and Meg, laughed and

chatted together while their small children wandered
happily amongst the group, their small hot hands
clutching filled lamburgers.

'Rob, meet Liz!' Molly was saying, and looking
towards the smiling young man with rugged features
and steadfast grey eyes. Liz found herself liking him at
sight. Instinctively she felt he was the sort of man you
could trust. Not like Jarrah, whose well-shaped lips said
one thing while his eyes signalled something entirely
different.

'Hi, how about me?' called the young 'copter pilot, a
slim youth with a cheerful grin. His appreciative gaze
rested on Liz's sun-flushed face. 'I'm Adrian. Do you
mean to tell me,' he marvelled, 'that you actually live
here and I didn't know? Why,' he demanded of the
others, 'didn't someone tell me there was a girl like Liz
around?'

Liz laughed, taking the plastic beaker of cool drink he
was handing her. 'Not for long! I've been training
Jarrah's thoroughbred for him and this is the day.' She
shrugged lightly. 'I hate to think what will happen to me
if I don't bring Mate in first to the winning post!' The
words were lightly spoken, but she threw Jarrah a
defiant glance.

He merely smiled, holding her gaze with his alive
hazel eyes. 'Not to worry, you'll make it!' He added in
his maddening laconic way, 'You and Mate together
it's an unbeatable combination!'

There was just no arguing with him on this particular
point, she thought irritatedly. He simply refused to
entertain the slightest possibility of failure. She pulled a
mocking face at him, but he only grinned again.

As she went to seat herself on the fringe of the group,
Adrian hurried after her, but in a flash he was beaten to
a seat at her side by Derek on one side and Wayne on
the other. Molly smiled across at Adrian, her eyes

twinkling. 'You've got to be quick to get anywhere near Liz at a picnic,' she observed.

'You're telling me!' the young helicopter pilot agreed ruefully, 'and I can see why!' His glance rested on Liz. She was leaning back, supporting her hands on the rug, letting the wind, fresh and cool with its salt tang of the sea, play over her hot temples marked with a red line from the recent pressure of her jockey cap. 'So you're going to win your race today——'

Before she could answer, Jarrah's vibrant tones drawled, 'She's got her orders!' The lurking spark in his eyes warned her that he meant what he said. Beast! She could have wrung his neck! she thought vindictively.

Bridget, with the air of a star who finds herself being overlooked in the general conversation by a girl much junior to herself, said indifferently, 'Oh yes, Liz knows her job!'

It was Bridget's tone of voice rather than the commonplace words that sent Liz's temper rising. 'Stableboy, you mean?' she flashed back.

Bridget's green eyes opened wider. 'What else? I mean,' she pointed out calmly, 'you are, aren't you?'

Now was the time, Liz thought hotly, for Jarrah to come to her rescue, to tell everyone listening to the conversation that she was something a whole lot more than a menial worker on the station. Hadn't he told her so himself?

He merely gave a careless nod of his black head. 'You could put it that way.' He added cryptically, 'All I know is that I couldn't get along without her.'

Stung, Liz managed to hide the stab of pain that was quivering through her nerves. Snatching up her jockey cap, she pushed it down over one eye and affected a jaunty stance. 'When the big boss puts it like that . . . what more could a girl want?'

In the general burst of laughter she was careful to

avoid Jarrah's eyes. She just knew the derisive way he'd be looking at her!

Liz had to force herself to eat a portion of the generous helping of sliced mutton and salad that Molly had heaped on a picnic plate and handed to her. She was hoping no one would notice her lack of appetite, but she wasn't to be so lucky, for Jarrah's hazel eyes never missed a thing. Not when it concerned the fitness of his young rider, and especially today.

'What's the matter, Liz?' There was no avoiding his discerning gaze. 'Don't tell me,' he drawled, 'that you've got an attack of the jitters! I wouldn't have thought a beach race would worry you any. Got the feeling you were an old hand at the game!'

'Oh, I am—I am!' She forced herself to swallow another mouthful of food. 'I told you, I'm not hungry.'

'Don't let her fool you!' Bridget's light tone belied the gleam of malice in her eyes. She gave her throaty laugh. 'Can't you see she's trying to slim? Maybe she can't take the competition!'

Liz was taken by surprise by the unprovoked attack. She opened her lips, but before she could think up a suitable rejoinder help came from an unexpected quarter.

'Come on now,' came Rob's deep slow tones, 'that's not fair! You know it's not true!' His steady gaze rested on Liz's rounded cheeks and fresh young face. 'Reckon Liz is just about right——'

'For a jockey?' There was an unpleasant twist to Bridget's lips. The glance she shot towards Liz underlined the deliberate put-down. 'Don't jockeys have to half starve themselves?'

Liz, sparked to anger, said with feeling, 'I'm not a real jockey.'

'Really?' Bridget's cool assessing glance moved over Liz's silk jacket and matching armbands. 'You could

have fooled me. All I know,' her disparaging gaze
flickered over Liz's smoothly tanned face, 'is that if I let
my skin darken to that unattractive muddy colour I'd
lose my modelling job and my TV contract would be
cancelled right away. Luckily,' she flashed a smile
towards Jarrah, 'Jay likes me this way ... such a
change, he says, from the dried-up brown skins of the
women in this part of the world.'

Liz stole a quick glance towards Jarrah. Had he really
said that? It wouldn't seem so, judging by his expression
of surprise, although he made no comment. The next
moment she told herself it was just wishful thinking. He
thought Bridget was perfect, why fool herself into
imagining anything else?

'Would it matter,' Rob's calm tones broke the silence,
'if you gave it all away? The photographic modelling,
the good life, the lot?'

The query was so absurd that a chorus of incredulous
laughter went up from the group. Liz saw with surprise
that only Rob wasn't joining in the merriment. He
appeared to be waiting for an answer to his question, his
rugged face oddly serious.

'*Would it matter*?' Bridget's voice was tinged with
amusement. 'You'd better ask my publicity agents
about that one and see what they tell you!'

'I'm asking *you*!' There was an odd intent note in
Rob's deep tones.

'Ask a silly question,' Bridget tossed off scornfully,
'and you'll get a silly answer!' For a moment she held his
gaze. 'If you must know, it depends on anything really
super turning up to make it all worthwhile!'

Molly said laughingly, 'Like a Greek tycoon or an
American millionaire? Anyway,' her glance rested on
Bridget, who had moved to seat herself at Jarrah's side
and was nestling her flame-coloured head against his
shoulder, 'what's wrong with a Kiwi runholder? You

always told me you couldn't find anyone overseas to compare with the rugged he-man types you'd left at home.'

Bridget gave her husky chuckle. 'You might be right at that!' Then, with a toss of her head, 'I'll let you know!'

Liz's gaze was drawn to Rob and she took in the look of strain around his mouth. Put it down to his recent accident, she thought, for surely he couldn't care so much for Bridget that the pain showed. Or could he?

'Anyway,' suddenly Bridget was smiling, gazing provocatively towards Rob, 'the important thing is that you came to the races today—or was it just for the races?' Her eyes signalled a message. 'Admit it, it was to see me again, wasn't it?'

Adrian broke in in his boyish tones. 'Blame me for bringing him along. He was all against the idea, but I dropped in on him with the 'copter and managed to talk some sense into him.'

Bridget didn't seem to have heard him. 'You were coming anyway, isn't that right, Rob?' There was an odd intensity in her husky tones. 'Some special attraction?' Her gaze was fixed on his face as though Liz thought, puzzled, the answer were somehow important to her.

His shrug was noncommittal. 'You could say that. I feel a fool on these crutches, but I wasn't going to miss seeing Jarrah come in first on Sultan!'

'I get it.' Bridget's long lashes veiled her eyes.

Suddenly Liz caught Wayne's conspiratorial wink. His low tones were audible only to herself. 'That was a bit of a let down for our Bridget! She doesn't look too happy about it either. Oh well,' he grinned, 'you can't win 'em all!'

For once, Liz mused, Bridget's power to charm any male in her vicinity wasn't working. Funny, that . .

Something stirred at the back of her mind. The day of
Bridget's arrival at Hauturu she had enquired about old
friends in the district, and although she had tried to hide
her reaction, Rob's name had sparked an immediate
response, something that seemed much more than a
neighbourly interest. It was an impression that had
puzzled Liz at the time, but she thought now that had
there once been a love affair between the two it was over
so far as Rob was concerned. His closed expression
could not have spelled the position out more plainly.
Not that Bridget would take his offputting attitude to
heart. Why should she, when she was with Jarrah,
whom she preferred to any other man and who . . . loved
her? All at once the hard lump was back in Liz's throat
and she tried to swallow it away.

One only had to look at the other two to know how
they felt about each other. For Bridget was clinging to
Jarrah's arm, gazing into his face with an expression of
blatant possession, verging on desire, that made Liz feel
sick. A part of her didn't want to admit that she was
jealous of Bridget—and yet she couldn't keep her eyes
from straying towards them. Bridget, whom in the past
she had thought of as a girl entirely in command of her
emotions, was now looking flushed and excited. She
was snuggling up to Jarrah, laughing up at him as she
held to his lips the three-decker sandwich she had been
nibbling. Sick at heart, Liz wrenched her gaze aside and
looked towards Rob, and in that lightning flash she
glimpsed on his face an expression of desolation. He
met her eyes and for something to say she murmured,
'They look happy together, don't they?'

'Jarrah's got it made.' She took in the stern set of his
lips and the pain in his eyes, but she didn't ask him what
he meant. Besides, she already knew—the way in which
Rob was looking at Bridget, the anguish in his eyes. He
loves her, Liz told herself, and she knows it, and she's

deliberately making it plain to him that he hasn't a chance with her, not when she and Jarrah are so much in love. No doubt, she mused, a famous model such as Bridget would collect men's homage and love as other women collected jewellery, to feed her own vanity. If anyone got hurt in the process, it certainly wouldn't be Bridget!

It was with a sense of relief that Liz heard the announcement of the next race, the Allcomers' Handicap. Stockmen and shepherds got up to join the long line of holidaymakers who were awaiting their turn to put money on their favourite at the equalisator.

As Liz left the picnic party, Jarrah came to join her. 'Good luck, Liz. Don't forget, I'm counting on you!'

But now there was no pleasure in his attention. Any feeling he might have for her was strictly on a business basis, she'd known that all along, Yet somehow . . . She pushed her traitorous thoughts aside, glancing up into his strong face. And there was again the hopeless longing for him that there was no assuaging. Sick at heart, she was scarcely aware of the chorus of good wishes echoing around her.

'Don't look like that!' His husky tone was far too close to a caress for her tremulous state of mind. 'Believe me, you haven't a thing to worry about!'

Not a thing to worry about! If he only knew! Swiftly Liz pulled her thoughts together and forced her lips to a smile. 'I'm okay,' she told him.

'Sure?' His low tones were threaded with concern. 'You look so pale.' But she knew only too well that his concern was for the success of the chestnut thoroughbred she was riding in the next race. 'Liz——' He laid a hand on her arm and suddenly she was almost unbearably aware of him. The strong face, the well-muscled strength of his body and most of all, the low pitch of his voice that went straight to her heart. And it all meant nothing, nothing.

She flung herself free of his hand. 'You heard what Bridget said a while ago.' Frustration and anger made her lash out at him. 'How could I possibly look pale with this tough tanned skin of mine?'

Jarrah said very low, 'I know which of the two I prefer.'

Defeat and desolation flooding through her made her say with bitter irony, 'There wouldn't be much doubt about that, would there?'

There! Jealous or not, she had said it! What did it matter anyway? What did anything matter? Soon she would be leaving him for ever. If only the thought of never seeing him again didn't hurt so much.

'Not to me.' Lost in her thoughts, Liz was only half aware of his low tones.

Liz glimpsed the tethered horses through a veil of tears and as Jarrah left her to bring the light saddle from the Land Rover she dashed away the moisture from her eyes with the back of her hand. He fitted the saddle over the fluffy sheepskin on the gleaming chestnut back, and soon he and Liz were riding together along the wet sand as they joined the straggling row of horses and riders who were heading for the starting line.

When they reached the far end of the beach Liz recognised familiar faces among the crowd gathered there. There was no doubt that the group from Hauturu were giving her an enthusiastic send-off. Even Rob, balanced on his crutches, was amongst the laughing, excited group. And wouldn't you know, she told herself, tight-lipped, that Bridget would be in the forefront of the watchers? As Jarrah approached the group she ran to meet him, gazing up at him with the possessive triumphant look that Liz found so hard to take.

'You've got to come in first, Liz,' called Molly, her

round face reddened from the salt-laden sunshine. 'I've
got my money on Mate!'

Male voices joined in the clamour. 'That goes for me
too!'

'And me!'

'Atta girl!'

Although she smiled and waved Liz heard the voices
as from a distance, as if all this were happening to
someone else, another girl. Only Jarrah's low tones
reached her consciousness. 'Good luck, Liz!'

She couldn't meet his smile. She said thickly, 'I'll do
my best . . . not to let you down.'

'That's good enough for me!'

The next moment the starter's gun jerked her to
instant action. 'They're away!' The line of horses
became more spaced out as the roar of the crowd
merged with the thunder of hoofs. Liz, forced to the
outside of the group as Jarrah had been earlier in the
day, found herself at the water's edge, and soon she
could scarcely see ahead for the sea-spray flung up
around her by the hoofs.

A swift glance thrown over her shoulder showed her
that one horse had pulled out of the race and another
rider was having trouble with his mount. So far so good.

Then she left the closely bunched group behind and
minute by minute forged ahead until only a fraction of
space separated her from the two horses ahead as they
raced for the winning post.

'Come on, Mate!' A roar went up from the crowd
wildly waving from the grassy hillside.

'Give it all you've got, Liz!'

Flushed, with excitement pounding through her
veins, Liz crouched low over the saddle as she urged her
mount to a still faster pace.

She had all but reached the winning post when in a
split second everything seemed to happen at once. She

felt Mate stumble, then she was tossed high in the air. Sea and sky rocketed by in a moving kaleidoscope, then she was falling down, down through deep intense blackness. Then . . . nothingness.

At her side the bunch of horses thundered on, the galloping hoofs avoiding the small crumpled figure lying motionless at the edge of the waves. But Liz, deep in merciful oblivion, knew nothing, felt nothing.

At first when she drifted back to consciousness Liz couldn't figure out her surroundings. Familiar surroundings . . . and yet . . . Why was she lying here in bed wearing a pink silk jacket? And why this dull ache at her temples as though someone had clobbered her over the head?

'Liz, my darling—you're awake!' The urgency and deep relief that threaded the masculine tones sparked a memory. Not Jarrah, though, the random thoughts flitted through her mind. It couldn't really be Jarrah's voice. He wouldn't be concerned about her, whatever it was that had happened to her. She had always known that he wasn't interested in her, not in the man-and-woman way she wanted him to be. It was only in dreams he would speak to her in that special deep *caring* way, the way of a man speaking to the woman he loved.

Slowly she raised heavy-lidded eyes, her blank gaze meeting the anguished glance of the haggard-eyed man who was bending over her. Hazily her thoughts drifted. Jarrah. If this were a dream she wanted to keep it that way. No Bridget, no one else in the room, just Jarrah in this strangely exalted tender mood, and herself. This couldn't really be happening. Not Jarrah, looking like this, his lean face dark-shadowed as though he hadn't shaved for ages, his eyes dark-ringed, his hair tousled as though he had run his fingers through and through it, as if he were worried sick about something—or someone.

And the way he was gazing at her. It was unbelievable that he was looking at her—that way.

'My darling——' Now she knew she was dreaming. In real life things didn't happen this way, not Jarrah clasping her hands in his tight grip, his deep tones hoarse with emotion. 'You're going to be all right.' He was raising her fingers to his lips. 'The doctor warned me,' he said on a deep breath of relief, 'that there was a chance of serious injury from that knock you took on the head, but if you came out of the concussion within forty-eight hours you'd be all right. And you have! You have!' The light that had flashed into his eyes sent excitement tingling through her veins. 'Liz,' he murmured brokenly, 'if you only knew!'

'Knew?' She could scarcely get the word out, for he was cupping her face with his hands, gazing down at her as if she were someone who was immensely important to him.

'You don't remember?' he urged gently. 'The beach races——'

The races! Realisation came flooding back to Liz's mind. 'Mate?' she whispered, her eyes wide and anxious. 'We were going so well and then he—crashed——' All at once fear threaded her tone, 'He's all right, isn't he? He's not——'

'Relax, honey.' Jarrah's voice was gentle. 'Not his fault that he put his hoof in a hole in the sand covered by the tide. He was up on his feet again in one minute flat, but you——' his voice thickened, 'you bailed out and hit the sand!' His eyes went dark and all at once his voice throbbed with emotion. 'Thank heaven you didn't tangle with the horses. All those hours,' she could scarcely catch his low tones, 'not knowing ... My darling,' he carried her fingers to his lips, 'don't ever put me through that again!'

A little of Liz's old spirit was coming back. It had

something to do with the warm soft expression in his
eyes. 'I don't suppose,' a teasing smile curved her lips,
'I'll ever get the chance after what happened. I didn't
even win your race for you!' All at once memory pricked
her to painful awareness. 'And anyway,' her eyes
clouded, 'I'm going away.'

'*No!*' There was something in Jarrah's deep tones,
husky with emotion, that sent a sudden dizzy happiness
shooting through her. He bent to take her in his arms
and her pulses raced at the contact. The supple strength
of him, the warm pressure of his hard-muscled body
against hers, the low pitch of his voice. 'Don't go—ever.
Stay here with me. I love you so.'

'I love you,' she whispered, 'I always have.' She gave
a shuddering sigh, then his mouth was seeking hers,
setting her pulses on fire.

His lips caressed her mouth in a tremulous kiss that
sent tremors running through her body, then the
pressure of his lips on hers deepened, the world around
them fell away and there was nothing but the wild sweet
ecstasy.

Jarrah's deep caressing voice was music in her ears. 'I
guess it took the accident to make me realise that you
mean everything to me. You're my life, Liz. I can't live
without you. I've loved you right from the start—and I
fought against it like hell!

'All these hours,' she could scarcely catch his low
tones, 'waiting here for you to come to, not knowing if
you were badly hurt, and all the time, just one thing on
my mind. Will she be all right, and if she is, does she feel
for me the way I do about her? There've been times
when I could have sworn,' gently he ran his fingers
down her pale cheek, 'and other times when I called
myself all kinds of a fool for hoping——'

Liz stirred in his arms. 'You weren't, you know. It
was just——' She raised blue eyes, clear as a child's, to

his face. 'I thought you couldn't stand the sight of me.'

Gently he pushed the damp hair back from her forehead. 'I fought against loving you all the way. Putting the blame on you for the break-up with Brooke, not taking your word for what had happened.'

Secure in her newly found happiness, Liz threw him a mischievous look. 'What made you change your mind—about me?'

His arm tightened more firmly around her shoulders and he dropped a light kiss on her nose. 'You, my love! Getting to know you, realising you just weren't the sort of girl who would let anyone down. Not you, Liz!' The warmth in his tone sent her spirits soaring.

Her eyes glimmered up at him. 'A woman of principle?' she mocked softly. 'Is that it?'

'*My* woman! The one I love. The girl who means more to me than anyone else in the world. Stay here with me, Liz,' Jarrah's voice throbbed with emotion, 'say you'll stay here with me for ever!'

When as last he released her she was flushed and smiling. Suddenly she was feeling so well. It was like starting to live again—with Jarrah! 'Is this really happening?' She was speaking her thoughts aloud. 'You know, I was so sure that you and Bridget——' She raised puzzled eyes to his face. 'Especially on the race day. Why was she all over you like that?'

He laughed, fondling her hand. 'Took you in, did it? That show was put on by Bridget for Rob's benefit, the idea being to make him so mad with jealousy he'd forget everything else and give in.'

She said bewilderingly, 'Give in to what?'

'Her proposal, that's what! I promised to keep things to myself, but that's all over now. The thing is that Rob and Bridget fell in love on that stay he had in London a while ago. It was the real thing for both of them, but there were snags. Bridget's an out-and-out career girl and always has been. She made it fairly plain to him that she loved him a lot, but love was one thing and work was another and she wasn't giving up the career she'd built up over so many years for life on a New Zealand sheep station. Not even for him! He was feeling pretty low when he took off for home in a hurry.

'But the moment he'd left England Bridget began to have second thoughts about her big decision. She wrote to Rob telling him she had changed her mind about their future together, but he didn't answer the letter.

'The break out here at Hauturu was her excuse for seeing him again and trying to make him believe she meant what she'd said in the letter about giving up her old life and starting a new one with him. Then when she found out about his accident she felt that fate was playing into her hands. This was her big chance, she told me, to give Rob a practical demonstration of what a great wife she would make him, primitive conditions and all!'

'But he——?'

'Didn't buy that theory! You've guessed it. He couldn't or wouldn't believe that she could change her mind so suddenly. In his view the marriage was bound to flounder, if it lasted any time at all. And by that time Bridget would have said goodbye to her chances of work overseas.

'All that cooking and cleaning she did at his run-down old house didn't impress him at all. And even when she let on to him that she had only a few days left here it made no difference. Oh, he loved her as much as ever, he couldn't hide that, but he wasn't going to ruin her career, let her in for a way of life she would come to hate. And nothing she could say to him could convince him otherwise.

'By then Bridget was feeling fairly desperate about things. The beach races was the last chance she had to change the ideas he'd got into his head about her. And time was running out fast.'

Liz was having difficulty in concentrating on his words. Somehow Bridget didn't seem of importance to her, not any more. Not with Jarrah's arms around her, holding her close, so close. 'Time?' she murmured.

'That's right. A few days ago Bridget got a long-distance phone call from London that really put her in a flap. The TV movie she'd arranged to appear in was being put forward by some weeks and if she wanted to take advantage of her big chance in that line of work she had to be on the London plane this weekend. For her it was either let the plane go—or Rob. And at last she got her priorities right.

'She and Rob had said their goodbyes to each other the day before the beach races and she got a shock to see him turn up there. He soon made it plain, though, that he hadn't changed his decision about their future together. That's why she lashed out at you at the picnic lunch and threw her arms around my neck in a last-ditch attempt to make Rob jealous. And then——'

'You'll have to fill me in,' said Liz. 'That's all a blank to me.'

'My darling, as if I didn't know!' Jarrah's voice broke and once more his lips sought hers in a lingering caress. 'When you were tossed off Mate,' he went on after a moment, 'it opened my eyes to a lot of things I'd been blind to before. Made things happen with Rob and Bridget too. Even Rob couldn't hide his feelings for Bridget any more,' his lips quirked, 'although she had to tear up her TV contract under his eyes before she managed to get the message through to him. She's over at his place now, letting him into her latest project. Seems there's opportunity in this country now for exclusive designer clothes and Bridget's all set to design and promote garments made from New Zealand wool—

sheepskin-lined jackets for South Island wear and new season's knitwear, all distributed under the BRIDGET label. She's planning to work from home, aiming for the retail markets in Sydney and Melbourne as well as this country. Rob's accountancy experience will come in handy there. By the way, Bridget's been ringing through every hour on the hour hoping to hear you're off the danger list.'

'Oh!' Somehow it was easy now to forgive the other girl for the sharp words Bridget had flung at her in the past. 'Hadn't you better——'

'Now now!' Tiny points of light glowed in Jarrah's hazel eyes. His voice throbbed with emotion. 'We've got more important things to do, like setting a date for our wedding. Marry me, Liz . . . say you will!'

The touch of his seeking mouth on hers stopped the words on her lips, but her ardent response to his caress left no doubt at all of her answer.

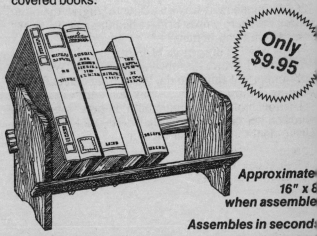

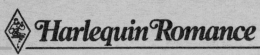 **Harlequin Romance**

Coming Next Month

2857 A MAN OF CONTRASTS Claudia Jameson
All signs point to a successful union when business owner Elaine marries a widower with a small son. When she becomes convinced he's still in love with his first wife, she faces the future with dismay!

2858 KING OF THE HILL Emma Goldrick
Marcie regards the Adirondacks mountain cabin she inherited as a needed resting place, until she becomes involved in a family feud started by her late uncle. Even worse, she fights with the one man she could love.

2859 VOYAGE OF DISCOVERY Hilda Nickson
Tha Canary Islands cruise is a new experience for Gail—a pleasant shipboard romance would top it off. But falling in love is a waste of time when the man in mind is not only uninterested but engaged!

2860 THE LOVE ARTIST Valerie Parv
Carrie sees famous cartoonist Roger as fancy-free and irresponsible, just like her father, who'd abandoned his family to pursue art. No way will she consider Roger as a husband.

2861 RELATIVE STRANGERS Jessica Steele
Zarah travels to Norway to unravel the mystery surrounding her real mother. She is shocked when she is regarded as a gold digger even by the one man she can turn to for help—and love.

2862 LOVE UPON THE WIND Sally Stewart
Jenny's quiet London life is disrupted when her lawyer boss's divorced son asks her to be his secretary. His second request is even more shattering—to be the wife he needs as a respectable candidate for Parliament!

Available in August wherever paperback books are sold, or through Harlequin Reader Service.

In the U.S.
901 Fuhrmann Blvd.
P.O. Box 1397
Buffalo, N.Y. 14240-1397

In Canada
P.O. Box 603
Fort Erie, Ontario
L2A 5X3

Take 4 best-selling love stories FREE
Plus get a FREE surprise gift!